Real Bitches Do Real Things 2

By

Keesh

Felony Books, a division of Olive Group, LLC,
P.O. Box 1577, Belton, MO 64012

Copyright © 2017 by Keesh Washington

ISBN-13: 978-1-940560-29-8

Felony Books 1st edition February 2017

10 9 8 7 6 5 4 3 2 1

Manufactured in the United States of America

For information regarding special discounts for bulk purchases, please contact Felony Books at felonybooks@gmail.com.

Text **JORDAN** to **77948**

And stay updated on all of Jordan Belcher Presents' *newest releases, free giveaways,* and *special promotions!*

"Real niggas let real bitches come first/ real bitches been bad bitches from birth."
—Nicki Minaj

CHAPTER 1

California Hospital Medical Center
Los Angeles, California

Detective Matt Figg squeezed out of the elevator doors before they came all the way open. The slack of his trench coat belts flopped around behind him as he stalked up to the nurse's station.

He flashed his badge at a blonde. "What room is Hershey Moore in?"

"Four-oh-six, sir." She pointed for him also. "Right at the end of the hall."

"Thank you."

Figg didn't knock. He pushed the door open to his suspect's hospital room and barged in, then suddenly stopped. He wasn't all that surprised by what he was seeing happening in here—this was Hershey Moore, after all, leader of the Crenshaw Mafia—but Figg didn't want to come any closer.

Keesh

A partially naked Black woman with perspiring almond-colored skin was riding Hershey as he lay in bed gripping her enormous rear-end. His fingers were clawing into her booty meat, as if he was hanging on for dear life. The woman wore a red wig, and it swept across her shoulder blades as she bounced on top of him merrily, the tips of the fake-colored hair stopping just above the tiny cursive "Crenshaw" tattoo. She must have picked this hair length so it wouldn't cover the ink. She was a proud, tatted-up female gang banger.

"*Yes, daddy, yes,*" she moaned quietly.

Figg's sexual masculinity made him hesitate. He observed wantonly for a moment, as the beautiful woman did her best to please his suspect. Her body was exquisite, almost too nice on the eyes, certainly too much for Figg to handle during off-duty hours. Actually, any girl was too much for him right now. Lately, only one woman consumed him, and it had nothing to do with sex. And that woman was Neeta Bryant.

"Forty-five more seconds," Hershey said to Figg. The Crenshaw girl looked over her shoulder, surprised to see a white man watching her fuck. She started to get up, but Hershey held her there and pumped harder. "Thirty seconds. You can count down for me if you want to."

Figg grabbed the girl by her arm and ripped her off of Hershey's lap. She got the picture then, snatching her arm free and picking up her clothes. She called Figg a *pig* under her breath, as she pulled her black thong up her shiny legs.

"And don't ever put yo hands on me again," she snapped.

Hershey looked irritated too. "You couldn't wait twenty more seconds?"

"No, I couldn't. Sorry." Figg held the door open as the lady in the purple wig walked out of the room. He shut the door behind her, then he took off his trench coat and draped it over his arm as he had a seat in the chair beside Hershey's bed.

Hershey had gauze taped to his face, and that matched up with the story Neeta told Figg about Hershey taking a bullet up close and personal. But she had fed Figg so much bullshit during that interrogation that it was impossible for him to know what else was truth. That's why he was here.

"Who tried to kill you, Hershey?"

"Why should I tell you? Huh? I was having a perfectly good time with a special young lady and you turn her away. Then you got the gall to ask me for some information? Where's the hospitality?" He smiled a little. "Get it? Hospital. Hospitality."

"You owe me."

"No, I don't."

"Yes, you do," Figg replied.

Keesh

"How long are you gonna hold that over my head? I was a teenager, detective. And since then, I've given you tons of bad guys. Crips, Pirus, *Sureños*, Folks, even a couple of them Temple Street muthafuckas. My debt to you is paid."

"Not until you get out of the life."

Hershey picked up a large Styrofoam cup and sipped from its straw. It smelled like liquor. "You're a piece of work, my friend."

"I'm aware of that," Figg replied stoically. "You know, you never told me why you were willing to take the fall back then. You wouldn't owe me right now if you would've just came clean from the beginning. And they would've tried you as an adult. I never understood it."

"I never told anybody my reason behind it. And I'm proud of that."

"Tell me, Hershey. Tell me why you were willing to go to prison for a crime you didn't commit. You were just a boy."

"You really wanna know, detective?"

"I do."

"Okay." Hershey set his cup down gently. "I wasn't a boy. I was 16 years old, and over in my 'hood growing up that's the age you start becoming a man. I wanted to be a man, or 'the man,' so bad back then. And prison didn't scare me ..." He cleared his throat. "I'ma start at the morning of the murders, okay? Bear with me as I try to remember all the details ..."

14

CHAPTER 2

Crenshaw High School
1994

Hershey liked to sit in the back of the class so he could send texts secretly, and also because rival gang members—there were several here at Crenshaw High—wouldn't be able to sneak up on him without being seen first. He would look up every now and then as a precaution and also to pretend he was paying attention to the bulletins on the chalkboard.

Sometimes it was enough.

And other times the English teacher, a white woman named Mrs. Robin Shulte, would catch him mid-text.

"Hershey, are you on that damn two-way again?"

Hershey looked up. "Yeah, I'm almost done. My thumbs keep hitting the wrong letters."

A few of his classmates chuckled.

"I didn't ask you if you were almost done," Robin said. She walked up close to him and held out her hand. "Give it here."

Keesh

"Nah, hold up baby. I gotta let my weed plug know where to meet me after school."

More classroom giggles, because they didn't know he was serious. Hershey stayed in contact with his supplier every few days, because that's how often he sold out of drugs. He had been hustling since he was nine.

"Give it here now."

"Just a few more words, Ms. Shulte. You're pretty good at spelling, right? How do you spell marijuana?"

More laughs, and Robin silenced her students with a swipe of her finger. Then she put her hand flat on Hershey's desk, the other still held out for him to drop his device in her palm. "Either hand it over, or get the hell out of my classroom."

"Fuck it, I'll just put *weed*. I know how to spell that." He typed a little more.

Then Robin snatched his two-way. "Get out!"

Hershey gave her a confused look, as if he felt that she had just overreacted. Some of his classmates looked on with anticipation, others even looked scared—for their teacher. They knew Hershey had been a Crenshaw Gangster since he was born.

"Get out!" Robin ordered again.

Hershey did the opposite of what everyone expected him to do. He got up and started walking out of the class. A couple girls said, "Bye, Hershey," and he responded with a presidential wave of his hand and a smile. The class shared another laugh before he closed the door behind him.

Leaning against the wall in the hallway, Hershey started thinking about the dress Mrs. Robin Shulte was wearing today. It was red, the color of sex, and it fit her tighter than the clothes she had worn at the beginning of the year. In Hershey's opinion, Robin was venturing more and more into the land of the provocative. Her heels had gone up an inch or two here lately, buttons on her shirts were left undone, and she had gotten fancier with her choice of lipstick.

Hershey had noticed. And it seemed like she wanted him to notice.

When she'd walked up to him demanding his two-way pager just minutes ago, her big breasts had been smack dab in his face. She wanted him to get a close-up and to smell her new perfume. It was a wonderful scent, the best shit Hershey ever smelled in his life. His classmates thought she was being strict on him, but she really had been flirting.

She was a teaser.

"I'ma tear that old pussy up the first chance I get," Hershey said to himself, then waist-pumped the air like a kid. "Then I'ma skeet this Crenshaw sperm in her face. I bet she never fucked a gangster before."

A half hour later the class bells went off and students started filing out of their classrooms in herds. Hershey went back inside his class to grab his books and get his two-way back.

Keesh

"Can I talk to you for a minute?" Robin asked. She was perched on the edge of her desk, ankles crossed. She held his two-way pager in her lap protectively, as if she wasn't giving it back unless he agreed to talk to her. "It'll only take a minute, Hershey."

He smiled inside. *She wants some private time with a G,* he thought. He sat down on the desk next to her—intimately close—and she didn't move away.

"Wussup, Robin?"

"Call me Mrs. Shulte, please."

"Sorry."

"Why do you always try to press my buttons? Is it just to get laughs from your classmates?"

Hershey shrugged.

She said, "I've been hearing around school about your extracurricular activities in your neighborhood. Are you in a gang?"

"Who's not in a gang?"

She frowned. "I've seen your test scores and it's clear to see that you're a smart young man. One of the smartest 16-year-olds I've ever had the pleasure to meet. But when you skip class and don't show up or don't turn in assignments I'm forced to give you zeroes. I wanna see you excel in life, not spending your time pleasing a gang that's gonna get you killed or thrown in jail forever. I want to see you graduate."

Real Bitches
Do Real Things 2

And I wanna see you naked, Mrs. Shulte.

Hershey said, "Thank you, Mrs. Shulte."

"Do me a favor, will you?"

"Yes, ma'am."

"Come over to my house tonight. There's a man I want you to meet. He's a gang prevention mentor who recently got out of prison. I think he can change your life around and put you on the right path."

Hershey sort of blanked out after *come over to my house tonight.* Did that just come out of her mouth? He'd been half-ass fantasizing when he thought she'd been purposefully dressing sexier to get his attention, but now he was for sure he'd been right on the money this whole time. She wanted the same thing he wanted. She was being blatant with her shit now.

Mrs. Shulte really wants me to fuck!

"Tonight?" Hershey asked, to be clear he'd heard right.

"Yes, tonight." She tapped his two-way, which was still resting in her lap. "I'm keeping this for collateral. If you show up and listen to the gang prevention mentor with honest interest and respect, and give feedback from the heart, I'll let you have it back. Deal?" She held out her manicured hand.

Hershey shook it firmly. "Deal."

19

Keesh

***

Hershey showed up at her doorstep in a black Adidas sweat suit, an outfit that was easy to come out of. His hair was cut and lined up, his breath smelled good, his white shell tops were dirt-free—he was ready to smash some punani.

Checking himself over one last time, he knocked on her door.

Mrs. Robin Shulte pulled it open, smiling at him. "Hey, you made it. Come on in."

Hershey stepped inside, eyeing what she had on. Blue jeans, a red Los Angeles Angels shirt, frumpy white tube socks—not even close to being eye-catching. Hershey expected her to answer the door in some sheer lingerie with a cut-out crotch. Either that or wearing nothing at all. Right now he wasn't impressed in the least. She was slumming it.

"You look nice," she said.

"You do too," he lied.

"Follow me."

"Yes, ma'am."

He did, looking at her butt the whole way. It looked better at school, he thought, more round and meaty than it did now (she had on a poor choice of jeans), but he was still excited to be here. If he didn't get past first base today, he could still say he'd been inside Mrs. Shulte's house. It smelled thick in here. It didn't stink; it just felt like there wasn't as much oxygen floating around as there should be. Maybe she'd just finished cooking or washing clothes.

"Hershey, I'd like you to meet Douglass Boyle, otherwise known as Crenshaw Doug." Robin was referring to the impossibly large man sitting at her dining room table. "He just got out of prison," she said. "Inside the walls, he changed a lot of people's lives. That was his job, to mentor the lost. His official title is gang prevention mentor. But he likes to call himself—"

"The Boss of the Wayward," said the big man, standing to his full height. He was just as tall as the chandelier hanging over the dining room table. Hershey was tall himself, but this man had him beat by at least a full foot.

Hershey was suddenly nervous. Not because he felt in danger, but because all his life he'd heard that the man who went by the street name Crenshaw Doug was his biological father. He'd only known him by name, never met him in person—until now.

This is my father?

"Listen to him, Hershey," said Robin. "He knows his stuff. What you're about to face with the gang life, Crenshaw Doug has already been through. Listen, learn, and ask questions."

Crenshaw Doug extended his hand to Hershey. "Kiss it."

"What?" Hershey said.

Keesh

"I'm the boss. Kiss the top of my hand. It's a sign of respect."

Hershey looked at Robin for help.

"Don't look at me," she said. "Look at him. He's here to help you. I saw something in you, Hershey, that reminded me of Crenshaw Doug. I knew once he was released, he'd be the perfect person to steer you in the right direction. Pretend that I'm not here. Interact with—"

"Shut the fuck up, Robin." Crenshaw Doug jiggled his hand at Hershey, reinforcing his command. "I said kiss this muthafucka, you little bitch! OG call!"

Hershey bowed at the waist and kissed the big man's hand.

Then Crenshaw Doug smacked Hershey upside the head and made him stumble a few steps.

"No violence," Robin warned.

"Didn't I tell yo fuckin' ass to shut the fuck up? This is gangsta business." Crenshaw Doug shot a mean look at Hershey. "Do you know what you just did? You kissed a grown man's hand, who you don't know from Adam. That right there tells me you're not cut out for this gangsta shit."

"But I do know you from Adam," Hershey said.

"You don't know me, nigga. I probably was in prison just as long as you been on this earth."

"You went to prison when I was five. You're my daddy."

Crenshaw Doug's angry expression sunk into a confused one. Then as he stared at Hershey longer, there was a sudden pop of faith in his eyes.

"Hole-lee shit ..."

Robin was just as amazed. "I knew there was something special about you two!" she chirped. "Oh my God, this is incredible! I get to witness this beautiful moment!"

Hershey wasn't sure this was something to be happy about. According to members of the Crenshaw Mafia and other niggas around the 'hood, Crenshaw Doug had physically abused Hershey's mother before he was born, up until his fifth birthday. Hershey didn't remember the abuse; he'd just heard stories. He also heard that Crenshaw Doug and another member of the Crenshaw Mafia committed a robbery/murder together. Crenshaw Doug was rumored to have snitched in the crime. And snitching meant death in the Mafia, which is why Hershey probably hadn't seen him around the neighborhood yet.

"Doug, are you okay?" Robin asked.

Hershey's father took a step back, bumping into the table and startling himself. Robin went to him, cradling his face in her hands and making him look her in the eyes to calm him down. Hershey watched his English teacher caress his daddy's face. He just knew they were fucking each other and that made him angrier than growing up with an absentee father.

Keesh

"I know this is a shock to you," Robin said to Crenshaw Doug in the soft voice of a paramedic. "But you have to calm down. Hershey needs you."

"God is a miracle worker."

"Yes, he is."

"I can't believe this." Crenshaw Doug seemed out of breath. He was suffering from shock.

"I can't believe it either," said Robin. "But you have to breathe normally, baby. Just breathe."

"That's my son!"

"Yes, it is. And this is the perfect time for you to talk to him."

Crenshaw Doug gathered himself, then took a giant step forward and took Hershey into his arms. Hershey didn't hug him back.

"I love you, son." Crenshaw Doug kissed him on the forehead. "This is a miracle. A goddamn miracle. You look good, boy."

"This is truly unbelievable," Robin gushed. "Hershey, is there anything you want to say to your father?"

"No, not really," Hershey said.

Crenshaw Doug released his son and turned his excitement on Robin. He kissed her, his hands wrapping around her waist and cupping her butt. She giggled and pushed him away.

"Not in front of Hershey," she said.

"Thank you for reuniting us," Crenshaw Doug said back. "I owe you even more now. You're my good luck charm."

"And you're mines."

Then the front door opened and their mood went from rejoiceful to pure panic.

"In the closet!" Robin said in a terrified shriek, as she pushed Hershey and Crenshaw Doug to the back of the kitchen, then to the hallway behind it. There was a closet here, which she thrust open. "Inside! Now!"

"I thought yo husband was out of town," Crenshaw Doug said.

"Me too! Get in there. Please. Hurry!"

Crenshaw Doug and Hershey squeezed inside the closet, and of course Hershey ended up jammed painfully against the doorframe and a line of itchy suits. When Robin slammed the door and plunged them into darkness, Hershey suddenly felt like he couldn't breathe.

"You okay, son?"

"No," Hershey said.

"Try to deal with it. We shouldn't be in here long. Robin will get us out of here as soon as she can. How's your mom?"

"On welfare."

No response.

Then, outside the door, they heard husband and wife arguing.

"Where the fuck is he?!"

"Where is who?" Robin asked.

"I know you got somebody in here. Where is he? I saw that old Chevy Caprice parked out front."

That's my car, Hershey thought.

The husband kept ranting. "I know you got one of those thugs in here, you lying bitch! I'll search this house up and down until I find him."

"I don't know what you're talking about, Travis. I'm here by myself."

There was an incredibly loud *smack*, and then the thud of someone hitting the ground. It was pretty easy to determine that Robin's husband had smacked her to the floor.

"Travis, no one's here. I swear to you!"

"You swear?"

"Yes! I would never cheat on you, Travis, you know that."

"But you never swear."

There was a heavy silence, then Robin started to scream and it was abruptly cut off with yet another *smack*, then another. Something crashed to floor and shattered, and Hershey remembered seeing fancy plates stacked on the dining room table and figured that's what he'd heard break. Next, there was a big thud that sounded close, so close that

Hershey felt the vibration. Robin must have gotten thrown against the other side of the closet wall.

Robin was getting her ass kicked.

"We're going out there," Crenshaw Doug whispered.

Hershey's expression disagreed, but it was too dark for his father to see his face. "We?"

"Yes, *we*. We're Crenshaw Mafia. We don't hide in closets and let men beat up women. C'mon."

Crenshaw Doug pushed the closet door open and the sudden onslaught of light was blinding. He stepped out, stumbling over a pair of rain boots. Hershey stayed in the closet, but he could see what was going on now—the slit in the hinged side of the door was that wide. Robin's husband, Travis, took his arms from around her neck and stood up straight, wiping his mouth with the back of his hand. He glared at Crenshaw Doug as if he wasn't surprised.

"He's a big ole boy, huh Robin? You went and got you the biggest Black dick you could find, I take it." Travis looked like one of those Wall Street guys—on a whole lot of speed. His hair was frazzled and his long-sleeved shirt was rolled up to the elbows. "What do you have to say for yourself, boy? Did you know you were fucking another man's wife?"

"I'm not your boy," Crenshaw Doug replied. "And yes, I did know I was fucking someone's wife. But to say you're a man is an exaggeration. *You're* the boy. And the worst kind at that."

Keesh

"You think you know me, motherfucker?"

"I know all about you. Your wife told me in visits and in letters. You can't keep a steady job. You're the least successful male in your family. You don't have any real friends. You wet the bed up until you turned thirteen. You have a nasty heroin addiction that led you to clean out your daughter's college fund. And I just saw for myself that you're a wife-beater. Let me see you try and beat me."

"Gladly."

Travis reached behind him and pulled out a revolver and—"Nooo!" Robin screamed—shot Crenshaw Doug square between the eyes. Hershey's position didn't allow him to see Crenshaw Doug's body hit the ground, but he heard it and felt it; the wood floor shook beneath his feet. He did see the gunflash though, and also the recoil that almost made Travis lose control of the weapon.

"What have you done?!" Robin screamed. "You just killed a man, Travis! Oh my God! Oh my God!"

"Shut up, bitch."

Travis shot her too. Another one shot/one kill.

Hershey clamped both hands over his mouth, trying not to make a sound. He was terrified, and the silence seemed like the loudest thing in the world right now.

Calmly, Travis pulled out one of the dining room chairs and had a seat. He pulled his belt through the loops and wrapped it tight around one arm. Then he pulled out a syringe and injected a narcotic into his veins. Hershey saw him gasp at the ceiling, his eyes rolling in the back of his head. He was "nodding." Hershey had served plenty fiends to know that Travis was high as fuck right now.

Then a moment later Travis placed the revolver's muzzle under his chin. He put his thumb on the hammer.

Click!

He hesitated.

And started singing the opening tune from Phil Collins's "In the Air Tonight."

"I can feel it ... coming in the air tonight, oh Lord," Travis sang. "And I've been waiting for this moment, for all my life, oh Lord. Can you feel it ... coming in the air tonight, oh Lord, oh Lord ..."

Boom!

A fountain of blood sprayed out the top of Travis's messy hair, and his dead weight fell over out the chair.

CHAPTER 3

California Hospital Medical Center
Los Angeles, California (Present Day)

Detective Figg had his legs crossed now, his trench coat laying over his lap. "So how did you end up with the murder weapon?"

"Well, it took me a while to work up the courage to come out the closet," Hershey said. "Probably a full fifteen minutes after everybody was dead. When I did come out, the first thing that caught my attention was that shiny revolver in Robin's husband's hand."

"Why would you steal a gun from a dead man who just murdered your father, your teacher, and then himself? That was just plain stupid."

"I was 16 years old, detective. At that time in my life guns were hard to come by. I was in the Crenshaw Mafia, but the OGs didn't give us BGs their best guns. We got the scrap steel, the shit that jammed up when you didn't want it to. So when I saw that revolver—a chrome Smith & Wesson .44 Mag—I had to have it."

The nurse came in and checked Hershey's vitals. She asked him if he was feeling any pain or any discomfort in his head and he didn't hesitate to say yes. Detective Figg wondered if he just wanted the hydrocodone pills she gave him. She left, and Hershey chased the pills with his cup of alcohol.

Detective Figg uncrossed his legs, leaned forward. "When the police caught you with the revolver, why didn't you tell them you weren't the killer?"

"I wasn't a snitch then," Hershey said. "I didn't want the same rep as my daddy. And just because I was Crenshaw Doug's son I had to really show-out for the Mafia—murders, robberies, whatever they asked me to do—in order for my brothers to know I wasn't cut from his cloth."

"You were gonna take the rap for something you didn't do because you didn't wanna be labeled a snitch? How can you snitch on somebody that's already dead? Any sane person would've thrown the blame at the husband in a heartbeat."

"But you're not understanding how big an opportunity that was for me. Those murders made national news. The public made me out to be a monster, but to the Crenshaw Mafia I was a hero. I was the one who killed a snitch, the little nigga who had the balls to kill his own daddy, and I didn't want to tell nobody the truth because I didn't want that praise to go away. The Mafia treated me like an OG from then on out."

"That's why you didn't cooperate with me when I was trying to prove your innocence?"

Hershey nodded, then took another sip from his drink. "Yep, that's it. But I'm glad you forced those people to do some more investigating. Gun powder residue and other forensic work freed me. I got the best of both worlds. I had my freedom, and the Mafia still believed I killed Crenshaw Doug. Even my momma was proud of me. She said my daddy deserved it."

"The fact that there was no sign of forced entry is what made me wanna dig a little deeper, instead of just blaming it on you like everybody else. That's the problem with a lot of our departments. We like to take the easy way out. But I'm one of the few guys who likes to get it right."

"My man," Hershey said, smiling.

Figg smiled back, then he got down to business. There was only one reason he was here. "Who tried to kill you? Was it Vida and the henchmen she got from Eddy?"

"No, it was not."

Figg's heart started beating faster. "Was it Neeta?"

"No."

"Tell me who it was, Hershey! Dammit! They found a lot of drugs in your house. If you don't cooperate with me, you're going away for life. You hear me? If you cooperate, I guarantee I'll get you a short sentence."

"I heard yall let Neeta get complete immunity. Why can't I get that?"

"No, we gave *Vida Benitez* immunity. There's a difference. We didn't know we had Neeta in our possession. And since Neeta made us all look like fools, immunity is off the table for everybody. All I can do is guarantee you less than five years. Help me, Hershey. I want Neeta bad. She embarrassed me. This is my last favor I'll ask of you."

"I've heard that before."

"Who shot you?"

Hershey took a deep breath. "Kamau Bryant."

"Kamau?" Figg's brow creased. "Why would he shoot you? I thought you guys were on the same team."

"In the beginning we were. But things changed."

"Okay, I wanna get this right. So I'm going to ask you a series of questions to determine what's real or fake from the story Neeta gave me. True or false answers, please." Figg looked him in the eyes. "Kamau sought you out on his own, without Neeta's assistance."

"True."

"Okay, on to the next one. Neeta met Vida Benitez in a—"

"Wait a minute. What did Neeta tell you about how me and Kamau met?"

"She just said he went out to Cali during college, yall had a meeting and you supplied him with drugs. Then she jumped to another part of her story."

Hershey scoffed, shaking his head. "So you believed I just sold some random college kid some cocaine?"

"She said that Kamau told you he knew Neeta, that's why you sold it to him. He used her name as clout."

"Nothing of the sort," Hershey said. "She's trying to hide the truth. I knew Kamau before college."

"How is that? Kamau is from Harlem."

"Ha! That muthafucka ain't from no damn Harlem. He probably never been to New York in his life. He's from Compton."

Detective Figg frowned. Neeta had him all messed up.

"Kamau wanted to be down with the Crenshaw Mafia. He wanted to be a cocaine cowboy. I accepted him, but I had to convince Murk and the rest of the Crenshaw Mafia brothers to let him in. And I did. But it proved to be a decision that I would soon regret."

"What happened?"

"Kamau crossed the line."

CHAPTER 4

Bellevue Recreation Center
Los Angeles, California, 2004

Hershey and Kamau had a couch to themselves, one of maybe eight or nine couches in this huge community center that Murk rented out. They were wearing black tailored suits with red bow ties and looked more like NOI Muslims than Crenshaw Mafia members. But this is how Neeta wanted all the members to dress for her Sweet Sixteen, so Murk enforced it.

"I can do the suit but not this bow tie," Kamau said, adjusting the knot but still not sure if it looked right.

"Leave the tie alone," Hershey told him.

"Why do we have to wear this shit?"

"It's what Neeta wants."

"Who the fuck is she?"

Keesh

"She's Murk's baby sister," Hershey explained. "Murk is the leader of the Crenshaw Mafia and what he says goes. I'm only second in command. These suits and ties make sense anyway, when you think about it. The Mafia is acting as security for this Sweet Sixteen, and security needs to dress alike."

"Which one is Neeta?"

Hershey looked through the crowd of teens on the dance floor. Neeta was easy to spot. She was the most gorgeous girl in the room, adorned in the best gold-diamond jewelry and a flowing Vera Wang dress that complemented her smooth chocolate skin. She had the lower skirt of her dress hiked up and was doing a little booty pop against a girlfriend.

Hershey pointed. "That's her right there dancing with her homegirl."

"Oh wow! She's cute as a muthafucka. Can you introduce me?"

"No."

"Why not?"

"Because Murk will kill you if he sees you trying to talk to his little sister."

"I'm not trying to fuck her. I just want her to know who the new member of the Crenshaw Mafia is. And I wanna meet the Mafia's first lady."

Hershey grunted. "C'mon."

Real Bitches
Do Real Things 2

Neeta had started taking pictures with a few friends, and behind the group of kids was a ten-foot tall champagne tower filled with real champagne (underage drinking, but Neeta requested it so Murk made it happen). Kamau pulled away from Hershey and jumped in one of the pictures, photo-bombing it, then on the next round of pictures he snuck his arm around Neeta's shoulder. Hershey quickly intervened before the photographer snapped the pic, pulling Kamau back out of the group.

"You're security!" Hershey berated him. "You're not here to celebrate."

"Neeta didn't complain," Kamau said.

"I don't give a fuck."

"You said you were gonna introduce me."

"After she gets done, I will."

But Neeta walked over to them before she was finished taking pics. "What's going on?"

Hershey introduced them. "Neeta this is Kamau Bryant, the newest member of the Crenshaw Mafia. Kamau, this is Neeta Lockett, Murk's little sister."

Neeta shook his hand. "Nice to meet you."

"Nice to meet you too."

She frowned at Hershey. "Why'd you pull him away?"

"Because he's supposed to be watching over you, not taking pictures with you."

"He's my age. He can have a little fun."

"No, he can't."

"If I say he can, then he can. It's my Sweet Sixteen and Murk said I have the final word on what goes on." Neeta grabbed Kamau's hand. "C'mon, Mr. Dreadlocks. You're with me tonight."

Kamau smiled at Hershey, as Neeta led him onto the dance floor.

Hershey thought they were just gonna fool around for the remainder of the song. But the two stayed on the dance floor together for the next track, and then the next track after that. It looked like Kamau grabbed her butt a time or two, but Hershey couldn't tell from where he was standing. He told himself that he was pulling the plug on the next song, if they tried to keep dancing together like they were a couple.

A firm hand slapped down on Hershey's shoulder, startling him.

"Are you not paying attention to what the fuck yo people is doing?!" Murk snapped.

Hershey stumbled over his words. "What ... what happened, what are you talking about?"

Murk pointed at Kamau and Neeta. "Why the fuck is the nigga you just brought into the Mafia freak-dancing on my baby sister?"

Taking a quick look, Hershey saw that Kamau had his hands on Neeta's waist, and his crotch area was actually making contact with her butt. Neeta was laughing, intentionally backing up into him while snapping her fingers to the melody.

"They just started doing that," Hershey said. "I'm about to go put a stop to it right now."

"He should've never been on the dance floor with her in the first place. Go get his ass, then I need both of yall to meet me in the locker room."

"Yes, sir."

***

Hershey had Kamau by the arm, leading him off the dance floor.

"Am I in trouble?" Kamau asked.

"Both of us are. C'mon."

Hershey opened the door to the locker room and pushed Kamau inside, then shut the door behind him.

There were already several Crenshaw Mafia members in here standing in a semi-circle, everyone identified by their black suits and red bow ties. Murk was the only one dressed slightly different. He wore a necktie, not a bowtie, and it was black, not red.

"Where are you from?" Murk asked Kamau.

"Compton," Kamau said. He looked over at Hershey, who was still holding onto his arm. He wanted Hershey to let go.

"You can let him go," Murk said, and only then did Hershey release him. Murk walked up close to Kamau, then straightened out the rookie's bowtie for him. "Do you know who I am?"

"Yes, sir. You're Howard 'Murk' Lockett, my boss."

"And did you know who that girl was that you were freak-dancing with a few moments ago?"

"Yeah, I just met her. She's your sister. Neeta Lockett."

"And what made you think it was okay to dance with my little sister?"

Kamau shrugged. "I don't know."

There was a long pause, Murk staring Kamau down, then the Crenshaw boss suddenly burst into laughter, and the other gang members started laughing too. Even Kamau began to feel the contagious laughter working up inside of him, and a smile of his own started to surface—until Murk smacked him across the face lightning fast.

Kamau took the smack like a man, immediately started to swing back but Hershey grabbed him.

"Don't!" Hershey snapped.

"You wanna hit me? Huh, nigga?" Murk taunted. "I need two more people to hold this nigga down."

As commanded, two big Mafia members stepped forward to help Hershey hold Kamau against the lockers.

Kamau didn't struggle, but he did say, "Nigga, you hit me first."

"And I'ma hit you last," Murk said, then punched Kamau in the jaw with a powerful righthand cross.

Kamau spit up blood, then kicked Murk in the knee and tried to kick him higher in the stomach but more Mafia members grabbed his legs. Then Murk really started to pummel him with punch after punch. Murk kneed him in the gut, punched him again—with a left and a right—then hit Kamau with a nasty uppercut that sent a swirl of blood flying from the new recruit's mouth.

"Let him go," Murk said, shaking the pain out of his right hand.

The members released him and Kamau fell to his knees. He was clutching his stomach, his head hanging low in severe pain, his dreads draping down like long black ropes reaching for the floor.

Murk looked at Hershey. "You brought this nigga to the team, so you finish beating him till he passes out. After that, if you still feel he's Crenshaw Mafia material, then I'll accept him. But make sure he knows the law. And law number one is: Don't fuck wit' Neeta." Murk snapped his fingers at the rest of the gang. "Let's get out of here, fellas. Let these two have some privacy. I gotta go show my baby sis her new Mercedes."

They started walking out, and as soon as they were gone Hershey bashed one of the lockers with his fist.

Clang!

It left a dent in the metal.

"You made me look like an idiot!" Hershey shouted at Kamau, who was trying to pull himself up on the bench. "Now I have to knock you out. I'ma make sure it's a one-hitter quitter, a'ight? Next time listen to me."

Kamau had just sat up on the bench when Hershey cocked back and swung a large fist at his head. Kamau was alert enough to weave backwards, and the momentum made Hershey fall to the floor. Kamau reacted fast, jumped up and kicked Hershey in the stomach. Then gave him another one for good measure.

"I don't let *nobody* put hands on me!" Kamau hollered.

"You gotta take an ass-whopping every now and then," Hershey moaned, clutching the pain in his stomach. "This is the Mafia, nigga. Help me up."

"Fuck that."

Hershey was hurting, but he still had the strength to reach inside his suit jacket for his pistol. He just wasn't fast enough. Kamau grabbed his arm and pried the gun from his grip, then stood back and pointed Hershey's own weapon at him.

"No, hold it!" Hershey said quickly, shielding his face with his forearms.

"I'm not gonna kill you, Hershey. You were just following orders. But Murk is a different story. I'ma show him a real gangster."

Real Bitches
Do Real Things 2

Kamau stormed out of the locker room, gun in hand. "No wait!" Hershey called after him. He struggled to his feet. "Kamau, get back here!"

CHAPTER 5

California Hospital Medical Center
Los Angeles, California (Present Day)

"So after Kamau took your gun, he just ran out onto the dance floor to catch Murk and started shooting at him?" Detective Figg asked with heavy skepticism. "Is that what you're telling me?"

"No, Kamau is smarter than that," Hershey said. "He saw Murk leading Neeta outside to her birthday car blindfolded, so he waited. He waited for them to drive off and he followed them in his own car. He gunned them down in traffic a few blocks away from the Bellevue Recreation Center."

"Neeta told me it was a Chevy Caprice that was following her and her brother. Didn't you own one of those?"

"I had a Caprice when I was a teenager, yeah. But at the time of Neeta's Sweet Sixteen, I was balling. I owned a Lexus. You only see me in luxury cars nowadays."

"I'm gonna have to verify that."

"I don't give a shit. You tryna say I'm lying about Kamau killing Murk? You think I did it? If that's what you think, we can cut this interview short right now."

"It's just my job to ask questions, you know that."

"Are you recording this?"

Detective Figg pulled a tape recorder halfway out of his trench coat pocket. It was blinking red. Then he tucked it back in. "Neeta told me you took her with you to kill Maseo 'Crendog' Hudson, a rival gang member, in retaliation for Murk's murder. Why would you do that if you knew that Kamau was the one—"

"It never happened."

Figg tried to read him, but it was hard to because his eyes were glassy from inebriation. "So Neeta lied about killing Maseo Hudson in your presence? She didn't tell me you killed him. She said she did."

"That sounds like a lie Neeta would tell. She wants the world to believe she's been a killer since she was sixteen. But it never happened."

"Tell me this then—if you knew Kamau killed Murk, why didn't you kill Kamau?"

"Because I brought Kamau in. If the rest of the CMG found out that Kamau was responsible, I would've gotten killed along with Kamau. So we kept it a secret."

"Didn't you get nominated as leader of the Crenshaw Mafia after that?"

"Yes." Hershey sipped some more alcohol. And that's all he had left—a sip. He took the lid off and downed some of the crushed ice. "And I deserved to be boss, if you ask me. I should've been boss before Murk because I was known for killing my daddy, a notorious snitch. I had more stripes than Murk."

"I take it Neeta doesn't know that Kamau killed her big brother."

Hershey laughed once. "Hell no she doesn't know. It was our little secret, until ..." He started coughing, so he pounded his fist against his chest until it stopped. "It was our secret until ..." The coughing returned, more pronounced this time. Hershey couldn't get it under control.

When Detective Figg saw blood spurt down on Hershey's chin, he shot to his feet. "Nurse! We need a nurse!"

CHAPTER 6

Western Honduras

Me and Kamau gained the trust of the indigenous people through joining in traditional dance and the customary sharing of povitica bread. With permission from an elder, one of the village boys, a scrawny lad named *Penang*, agreed to show me and my husband the way to the neighboring cocaine plantation. The only route there was through the forest, on horseback.

Penang's age was unknown. He had the skinny little body of a 10-year-old, but the assuredness of an adult man. I felt confident and safe following behind his horse with my own. I looked back behind me at Kamau—he didn't look so confident, or safe.

"You okay, baby?" I said to him, trying not to laugh.

"Neeta, you know I don't do horses. And they don't do me. This is unnatural for the both of us."

Kamau's horse was larger than mine, and thus harder to control. He went off the path twice, and Penang had to trot back and grab Kamau's reins, guide him back onto the narrow road.

I had asked Kamau if he wanted to trade horses before we left the village, but his pride wouldn't let him.

Penang wasn't wearing a shirt. His ribs were showing but I knew he was strong. Less than an hour ago he lifted a wooden cart by himself, so his uncle could knock the broken wheel off its axis. My spine would've failed if I tried that. What Penang did have on was cut-off jean shorts and thong sandals, with a pouch attached to a strap that was slung over his shoulder and down across his bare chest. The pouch was girl-like (it resembled a purse), but in his village it was masculine. His hair was boyish. Silky, black, and cropped.

Me and Kamau were dressed like the Americans we were. I had on a white polo shirt, brown cargo pants and sandals similar to Penang's, except mine were white and made in Italy. Around my neck was a chain with a Lady K'abel pendant I had snatched from Vida's dead body.

Kamau wore a black button-up with military-esque epaulettes, black jeans and black and gold Givenchy sneakers—he was my handsome, dreadlocked black knight, who didn't know how to ride a horse.

We trotted for about another mile, the canopy of umbriferous trees seeming to get lower and lower, forcing us to duck down and push leaves out of our faces. My horse snorted. You would think this path hadn't been traveled in years.

Real Bitches
Do Real Things 2

"We no cut trees because we no want plantation to be found," Penang said in his best English. "Trackers, hard to find it."

Then Penang suddenly pulled back on his horse's reins and his animal stopped. I copied him, and my horse halted too. Up ahead there was a dirt/rock path that sloped downward at a dangerous degree. I wasn't sure if our horses would make it.

"We dismount here," said Penang. "Passage unsafe for you two—"

"Whoa!" Kamau shouted.

I looked back and saw Kamau's horse charging forward. Then he galloped past me and his horse jumped down the rocky slope.

"Kamau, pull back on the reins!" I screamed.

"I did!"

"I go after him," Penang said, snapping his reins. "Yah!"

Penang raced down the slope after my husband, so I snapped my reins too—not as hard as Penang had—and I galloped down after them. It felt like gravity was trying to bump me off of my horse so I had to slow it down with a tug. I saw Kamau galloping down way faster than he should have been, maybe 40 mph, and then his horse suddenly dug its hooves into the dirt, and Kamau was catapulted into the sky.

Keesh

He was airborne for an eternity.

Then he landed on a bed of beautiful, tall green plant life—but it was still a terrible landing, as he fell *into* the bed of plants, disappearing inside the green, its branches cracking under his weight until he hit the dirt below.

I heard him cry out.

By the time I got to the bottom of the steep path, Penang had already dismounted and was pulling Kamau out of the matured plants, which were a whopping ten feet tall!

God, that had to be a painful landing, I thought.

"You okay?" I asked.

Kamau was dusting himself off. "I did that on purpose," he said.

I laughed.

Penang was inspecting one of the stalks that Kamau crushed. "We no stay long," he told us. "The Watchers will come if they see us."

It took a second for me to understand what the small Honduran meant. Then I looked around and realized we were here. We were surrounded by cultivated coca plants.

"Kamau, this is it!" I said excitedly, swinging my leg off the horse, dismounting. The ground was soft beneath my feet. "There's miles and miles of cocaine!"

"They make us work day and night," Penang said. "They cut down our coffee beans, make us grow coca. They want more and more coca."

Real Bitches
Do Real Things 2

They.

I knew who he was referring to. Penang and his fellow villagers were enslaved to this territory by the country's military. For decades they had been tilling this land against their will, the cocaine profit being funneled out of the region into the hands of a tyrannical general some fifty miles east. I knew the story before Penang told me. Vida Benitez, who was once my friend, had already explained to me the situation here in Western Honduras, because I forced it out of her, right before I murdered her in a car explosion. She and Eddy Galvan had tried to claim this land as their own and cut me and Kamau out of the distribution back in America. But me and Kamau had our own plans now.

"Why is no one working today?" I asked.

"One day in week we no work to honor Lady K'abel."

I touched the pendant around my neck, which depicted their ancient queen Lady K'abel. Vida didn't deserve to wear this.

Penang plucked two leaves from one of the stalks of a huge, healthy coca plant. He handed one to me and Kamau each. "Chew," he said.

I looked at Kamau and he looked at me. We were thinking the same thing. *Should we?*

"What the heck," Kamau said with a shrug, then popped his leaf in his mouth and started chewing.

Keesh

I did the same. After a while I started feeling a little tingling in my gums. Numbness was setting in.

"I feel it," I said.

"Me too," said Kamau. "I can feel it softening my muscle pain from my fall. This is the real deal."

"We're gonna be billionaires," I said to Kamau, smiling. "I wish Murk was alive to see this. He'd be so proud of me."

Kamau didn't respond. For some reason he always got quiet when I mentioned my big brother.

I know now wasn't the time to confront him about it, but I felt confident at this moment, here out in the middle of this unfamiliar wilderness. Maybe it was the coca leaf giving me courage.

"Kamau, why do you always—"

That's when a shot rang out and Kamau was knocked off of his feet.

Penang shouted at me. "Get down, *senorita!* It's The Watchers!"

I dropped to the dirt with Penang, then army-crawled over to my husband. He had his head lifted off the ground, trying to see the damage and stay low at the same time. He was clutching his ribs where he'd been sniped.

"Is it bad?" I asked him frantically.

Kamau groaned. "I think I'll live. It just took off some skin. Went in and out."

Real Bitches
Do Real Things 2

I helped him put pressure on the wound, as we heard a pounding of approaching horses. A group of older men in straw hats galloped up to us, billowing up clouds of dust. I started coughing, all of us did.

Then came that sound that was the precursor to death: *Click-clack. Click-clack.*

The men aimed rifles at us, while gripping their reins to keep their horses steady. I was just as afraid of getting shot as I was of getting trampled to death by hooves.

One of the men barked something in Spanish, and another one of the men hopped off of his horse and began to tie Penang's hands behind his back with old dusty yellow rope. Me and Kamau were next.

***

We had been taken north, into a wooden shanty with a corrugated metal roof that sat up on a hill overlooking the whole cocaine plantation. Standing side by side with our hands tied behind our back, me, Kamau and Penang stared at the man sitting behind his desk with his feet kicked up. The bottoms of his cowboy boots were black and worn.

He took off his straw hat and rested it on his desk. I could see he was going bald.

"You come into my land, try to steal my coca?" he asked, staring at us while chewing on coca leaves. There was a glob of green churning in his mouth. "You think I let you steal from me? Did Penang tell you who I am?"

Penang started to speak to him in Spanish but he cut Penang off with a wave of his hand. There were armed men standing behind us.

The man stood up. "My name is Israel Trevino. I am the overseer here. And you two are trespassing. Tell me why I shouldn't kill you both right now?"

"We're just American tourists," I said.

"American?"

"Yes, we were gonna pay Penang American money after he showed us where he and the rest of the villagers worked. It's for college research. Me and my husband attend Georgia State."

"Where's money you plan to pay?"

I reached in the big Velcro pocket on my thigh and pulled out a wad of rubberbanded twenties. Total, it had to be close to five hundred dollars. One of the men from behind snatched the cash from me.

"This is my land," said Israel, "not Penang's. You pay *me*, you understand?"

Kamau said, "We're sorry for trespassing, sir. May we please go so I can get this wound sealed professionally?"

"Just one moment."

One of the men stood in front of us and held up a Polaroid camera. He took our pictures individually, then tacked them on the wall where there were fifteen or so other Polaroids. Some of the pictures had red X's drawn through them.

"If we see you again on my plantation," said Israel, "you will earn an X. And trust me, you do not want an X."

He nodded at one of his men and we were cut free.

***

Back at the village, Kamau was graciously being sewn up by the village doctor, who looked to be nearly eighty years old. The doctor was bare-chested—most of the men here were—and he straddled Kamau's waist in a strangely sexual way, as he worked the thread and needle through Kamau's skin deftly. Kamau didn't look to be in pain to me, and that could be because the unorthodox healer applied some kind of powdery medicine to the wound beforehand, and made Kamau drink a bowl of clear liquid that my husband said burned his throat.

Afterwards, when night had fallen, Penang took us to a woman he was excited for us to meet. It would have been a long walk so Penang gave us a ride there in his uncle's cart. Me and Kamau sat comfortably in the cart's seats while Penang pulled us by horse. It was a bumpy ride, but the stars in the sky also made it a romantic one.

I didn't miss Los Angeles at all.

Keesh

The woman we were headed to meet was a *shaman* named Antebella who had agreed to tell our futures, Penang explained. When we got there she was wafting in the center of the lake completely naked under the moonlight. She was an older woman with saggy breasts and a long gray braid that disappeared underwater. Me and Kamau stood at the shoreline watching her waft about aimlessly.

"You must go in to meet her," Penang said.

"Go in?" I echoed.

"Yes, *senorita.*"

"Ladies first," Kamau said to me, and nudged me forward. My feet got wet.

"No, that rule only applies in America," I said back to him.

"You both go," Penang said. "But you have to undress first."

"We gotta get naked?" I asked.

"Yes. The water must stay pure."

Me and Kamau were no strangers to getting naked in front of people. Our first time having sex was in a Miami penthouse filled with our fellow college alumni. And tonight, I felt like being naked.

We took our clothes off in front of Penang, and I looked over at Kamau and suddenly realized how big his dick was. A silly, jealous thought nipped at me: *This Shaman lady better not try to touch it.*

I walked into the lake first. The water was surprisingly warm and soothing.

"It feels nice," Kamau said, wafting in after me.

"Yes it does," I said.

We held hands as we made our way over to the mysterious Antebella.

"Jealousy!" the old woman hissed at us.

I was startled. "What did we do?"

"Your minds are filled with *jealousy*. You must submerge."

Then it hit me what she was talking about. It was the thought I had before I walked into the water. *How did she know?* I wondered. *And if she really had powers, what was Kamau jealous about?*

Kamau looked at me with confusion, and I didn't want to tell him that I had a small thought of this lady checking out his package. I wasn't even a jealous person, and this lady wasn't even Kamau's type.

So I dunked myself underwater, and so did Kamau. I held my breath until all the negative thoughts were cleared from my mind, then I bounced up through the surface. I was soaked, and the moonlight made my breasts glisten.

Kamau came up for air after me. His dreads sparkled.

Pulling my hair back to squeeze the water out, I said, "Jealousy all gone."

"I'm good too," Kamau said.

Keesh

"Hands, please," said the shaman.

All three of us held hands, forming a small circle in the night. The woman chanted something under her breath and then looked at us both.

"I see the two of you in hut above the stars," she said. "Love was there. The beginning."

I understood her. "Me and my husband had sex for the first time in a Miami penthouse on South Beach. It was 40 stories in the air. Above the stars, so to speak."

She closed her eyes. "I also see another man. He not alive. He watches over you, Neeta."

"My brother!" I exclaimed. "I pray and talk to him all the time."

"He listens always."

I looked at Kamau in near tears. "Did you hear that? Murk hears me!"

My husband nodded, but didn't seem impressed.

"There is destruction in your future," Antebella snarled. It seemed like the water suddenly got warmer against my skin. "There will be *death*. There will be *sadness* and overwhelming regret."

"Who dies? How can we stop it?" I asked.

"I see a lot of lies and secrets," the woman hummed as if she didn't hear me. "Secrets and lies. If you wish to have everlasting union, the lies must be no more and the secrets must be uncovered."

This time I had no clue what she was talking about. "Me and my husband are always truthful with each other. We've lied and kept secrets from others but that's it. Right, Kamau?"

He didn't even look at me. He just nodded again. "That's right, Neeta."

CHAPTER 7

California Hospital Medical Center

Los Angeles, California (Present Day)

Detective Figg was worried after seeing Hershey cough up blood. He hoped his suspect could make it through this interview without keeling over and dying. The doctor told Figg it was okay for him to go ahead and continue the interview, so that's what he was going to do.

"I don't have very many questions left," Figg said with arms crossed, leaning against the room's window seal. "You okay?"

"Yeah, if you fill me up," Hershey said, shaking his empty Styrofoam cup.

"I can't do that, Hershey. You know I can't provide you with alcohol. Unless you want water or soda?"

"Bummer." He slammed the cup back down. "I'm okay. Get on with your questions. And you better get me a good deal in court. I wanna see you there in person when I get my sentence. I'm giving insider secrets right now so I deserve your presence."

"I'll be there."

"Good."

"Neeta mentioned some names to me, names of key players in you guys' operation. I need you to verify them."

"I'll do my best."

Detective Figg uncrossed his arms and set his palms down on the window seal. "Do you recognize the name Mark Corr as someone who buys cocaine from Kamau and Neeta?"

Hershey shook his head no.

"Are you sure? Neeta told me this Mark guy was from Chicago."

"Never heard of him," Hershey said.

"What about Ralph Cleary in Miami?"

Hershey burst into laughter out of nowhere, and then it quickly turned into a cough that he couldn't control. Figg started toward the door to grab a nurse but Hershey held up a hand, stopping him. A minute later Hershey seemed okay.

"Coughing hurts," he said.

Then the gang member must've remembered what made him laugh in the first place because he let out another chuckle, and just like before a cough seized him. Hershey quelled it quick this time though, and took a moment to take a few deep breaths.

Figg asked, "Was something I said humorous?"

"Oh yes." Hershey was smiling, shaking his head at the detective. "Neeta had fun with you."

"How so?"

"The name Ralph Cleary. It comes from her favorite book as a child, *The Mouse and the Motorcycle*. The mouse's name was Ralph, and the author's name was Beverly Cleary. That's where she got Ralph Cleary. She didn't give up her clientele. She made the name up."

"Do you think Mark Corr is a fake too?"

"I do now. What kind of tie is that you have on?"

Figg looked down. There was an "MK" printed on it, which stood for Michael Kors. He had a fleet of these neckties at home. He looked back at Hershey, his cheeks warming from embarrassment. Neeta had made up fake names on the spot. Figg said, "She also told me about Eddy Galvan. I know for a fact he's real."

"Yeah, she told you about him because you and the FBI are already on to him."

"What about The Queen? Kelly 'The Queen' Alex—"

Figg paused. He'd just realized where Neeta got that name from. His watch was an Alexander brand.

"She told you about The Queen?" Hershey asked.

"Wait, The Queen is real?"

Keesh

"Yeah."

"What's her name?"

"No one knows," Hershey explained. "The Queen is kinda like a myth in the drug world. Eighty percent of the cocaine in America supposedly comes from her. We tell our customers our dope comes directly from her, because it sounds good."

"I've never heard of her."

"I bet the FBI has. She's a Honduran legend."

Figg sat back down in his chair, on the edge of it. "Neeta mentioned Western Honduras, and Eddy and Vida starting a pipeline from there to here in America. What do you know about that?"

"Eddy talked to me about it. He had this big idea of taking over Western Honduras and cutting Kamau and Neeta out of the distribution process. I told him I'd think about it but didn't take him serious."

"I think Kamau and Neeta are gonna attempt to do what Eddy had planned—take over Honduras. I think she told me about it because she knows there's nothing I can do to stop her. It's out of my jurisdiction."

"That sounds like Neeta. Her and Kamau are intelligent and insanely bold people. I'll give them that."

"Tell me more about The Queen," Figg said impatiently.

"She's a myth."

"I still wanna know her story."

Hershey sighed. "A'ight. All I know is bits and pieces of it." His eyes wandered, as if he was trying to figure out where to start. "Before The Queen, there was The General, who was The Queen's father. The General was dishonorably discharged from the *Fuerzas Militares de Colombia*, which is the Columbian military down there. He killed a soldier in his division while high on opium. He beat the military trial because the soldier's body was never found, but they ended up kicking him out of the *Fuerzas Militares* and sending him back home to Honduras. He had trouble adjusting back to village life."

CHAPTER 8

Western Honduras
1979

General Vincente Magana had one hand on the wheel of his army green Jeep Wrangler, the other on the gear shift, as he traveled the bumpy road back home to his village located over fifty miles outside of Santa Rosa de Copán. He had a bunch of healthy hair still, and a full beard. Not common for a man of his age. He was 39. His forehead was pronounced, somewhat bulky, and he always appeared to be upset. And today he really was.

He'd been thrown out of his service branch and was now classified as a civilian.

That would fucking piss anybody off.

But he still had a single-action 9mm with a 10-shot mag strapped to his thigh. And he was still wearing his official fatigues as if he was still on active duty.

Keesh

With focused green eyes staring ahead, he pressed his heavy boot down on the gas, propelling the Jeep forward at a speed unsafe for a road as bad as this one. He wasn't in a rush to get back to his village. Rather, driving fast—feeling the wind against his facial hair, hearing overgrown tree limbs slapping against his windshield—just made him feel better, as if he was still in combat.

When he got to his village, he saw a ton of adults and kids with content faces working and playing on the land he grew up on. Every other person was barefoot and bare-chested, even a few women.

Nothing has changed, he thought, feeling ashamed of these people who were *his* people.

A skinny child ran up to his vehicle and he hit the brakes and instinctively touched his 9mm. On the battlefield, some-times kids were used as decoys, and some of them even had bombs secretly attached to their genitals.

"Hola, uncle," the boy said with a huge smile.

General Vincente Magana had never seen this child in his life, but assumed that he could possibly be his nephew by looking at his dominant forehead. Vincente had heard that his sister, Marissa Magana, had birthed many kids since he joined the *Fuerzas Militares de Colombia*. Every child in this village could be his kin.

Vincente said, "Take me to your mother," in the same hard Spanish tone in which he used to address his lower-ranked soldiers.

"*Sí*, uncle. May I ride with you?"

Vincente looked at the boy's underpants suspiciously. "No, you may not."

The boy still seemed good-spirited, and waved for Vincente to follow. The General did, crawling the Jeep forward from several paces back. He parked once the boy pointed to a small house with a straw-thatched roof.

Vincente hopped out of his vehicle and went inside.

And suddenly, seven or more children rushed him and hugged his legs. He began to panic, his eyes searching the room frantically for the enemy soldiers that would prove this was an ambush. But he saw none.

"Back up, scat!" his sister Marissa said to the children. They broke away, laughing. Then Marissa hugged Vincente warmly. "All the kids have heard stories of their general uncle. You're a legend here, brother. It's good to see you. Welcome home."

"Your children are dressed poorly," Vincente pointed out.

His sister grimaced. "We make due, Vincente. We may not be rich in clothes, but we have food and water and happiness. We have a thriving bean plantation grown on the richest soil in this country."

"How many *lempiras* do you bring in monthly from the bean plantation?"

"Let's not talk about finances, brother. You're finally home after many many years." She smiled, and was missing one tooth, a canine. "We'll have plenty of time to talk about other things. Right now we rejoice!"

"Father!"

Vincente spun around and saw a girl running up to him that almost made his heart stop. She looked so much like his beautiful wife Helinda who died from Chagas disease (a disease commonly found among the South American poor) a year after he had enlisted in the *militares*. When the teen-aged girl wrapped her arms around him and buried her face in his chest, he didn't feel any of the panic or anxiety he'd felt when the other village children attacked him. Now, he was feeling an emotion he hadn't felt since he returned to Honduras, an emotion he hadn't felt in over a decade.

He felt love.

And when he sniffed his daughter's hair, the scent brought back wonderful memories that were almost unbearable. His eyes began to water.

"Helinda, my queen," he croaked.

She looked up at him with the most vivid green eyes. "My name is Amelia, *papi.*"

He smiled. "Amelia ... my dear Amelia ..."

Real Bitches
Do Real Things 2

***

His daughter, Amelia Magana, wore a hand-stitched cotton sundress that looked and smelled like new material. He was glad for that, but would have liked to see her in diamonds.

She was leading him to the bean plantation by horse. They were riding the same Spanish thoroughbred, with Vincente in the back reaching around his daughter's small waist. She was gripping the reins, in full control of this large domesticated animal.

They trotted along peacefully.

"How do you like it here?" Vincente asked her.

"Um ... May I be honest, *papi?*"

"*Si.* You must always be honest with me."

"I hate it here."

"Why?"

"It's so slow, village life. It's the same thing every day. I've heard stories about all the places you've been and the riches you've seen and I have dreamed about being there with you. The closest I've been to city life is Santa Rosa, and every time we deliver beans there I want to stay. Have you been to the United States, *papi?*"

"Many times."

"Is it as beautiful as they say?"

"The cities are, not the people."

"Will you take me there one day?"

Keesh

"*Sí*, my lovely Amelia. I will grant all of your wishes if they are within my power. And my power exceeds most."

At the sight of the bean plantation, Vincente grunted under his breath. He wasn't impressed by the harvest. The soil looked improperly mulched and the land hadn't been weeded well enough, which had clearly effected the root systems. With as many people in the village as there were, this plantation should have been immaculate.

"What do you think?" Amelia asked her father.

"I think it's horse shit," replied General Vincente Magana, as he turned and spat on the ground. "How often do you all work this land?"

"Only a few days a week. And it's only just a few of us women that keep it up."

"This needs to be worked at least six days a week. *At least.* There should be miles more of crop."

"I agree," said Amelia.

"Who's in charge of the plantation?"

"Aunt Marissa. Do you want to dismount to inspect the field further, *papi?*"

"No. We head back to the village. I have a plan that will make us rich beyond our wildest dreams, a plan that will take you to America to not only see it, but to savor in its spoils. And it starts with a can of gasoline."

Real Bitches
Do Real Things 2

***

Fire. One of the biggest Vincente had ever seen. The whole bean plantation was almost ablaze, the heat making the stalks crackle and snap loudly.

Amelia was holding the gas can, astonished. "It's so pretty watching it burn," she said. "I didn't know it would be this cool to see."

"I once burned down a whole village," Vincente said, almost to himself. "The enemy was unprepared for it. They ran out of their homes in long underwear, and were shot down immediately. The ones who didn't have a chance to make it out the fire were burned alive. Women and children screamed and cried at a level I hadn't heard before. They sounded like demons."

"Did they deserve to die like that, *papi?*"

"It doesn't matter. It was war."

They watched the fire rage on. It had engulfed the whole plantation.

Amelia said, "Aunt Marissa will see the smoke and she'll come. She'll be upset with us."

"Let her come."

Not even a minute later they heard the galloping of approaching horses. They turned and saw several villagers crossing the pasture on horseback, Marissa leading the pack. She raced over, snapping her reins, but her horse reared up

77

on its hind legs and neighed at the onslaught of heat from the enormous fire. When its hooves stomped the dirt again, Marissa dismounted.

"How did this fire start?" Marissa asked with alarm, her glare jumping between her brother and her niece.

Amelia held up the gas can. "This was all it took, auntie."

Marissa snatched the gas can from her, then smacked her and cursed her in Spanish. Vincente shoved his sister backwards.

"I ordered Amelia to burn it down," said The General.

"Why, brother?!" Marissa's eyes went wild. "This is how we feed our village!"

"There's a new way—a better way—to feed everyone."

"And what way is that? Burn our own crops? Vincente, did the *militares* drive you mad?"

"No, my dear sister. Starting now, this soil will be used for the raising of coca plants. We will extract and distribute the psychoactive alkaloid known as cocaine."

***

It took months to get the villagers to work together in a cohesive, timely manner. But Vincente whipped them into shape—literally. He had to pull off his belt many times and slap his nephews—and other non-relatives, young and old—across their skinny backs when they didn't plow the land to his liking. He taught Amelia how to oversee them, because he believed she was too intelligent to partake in such meaningless labor as farming. She got the hang of being in charge.

One day, in the middle of the field, Amelia caught her Aunt Marissa sitting down in the dirt.

"What's wrong, auntie?"

"I'm done," the woman grumbled. "I'm sick of this."

"But the sun is still out and will be out for three more hours."

"I said I'm done!"

Amelia frowned at her.

"This is crazy," Marissa said. "Our whole village will be thrown in prison for growing this crop. And if the *policia* don't get us, the cartels will wipe us out. I'm done with this nonsense. I want no parts of it."

"Get up, auntie."

Marissa looked up. "Are you ordering me?"

"Yes."

Marissa laughed, but there was no humor in it. "You nor your father are my boss. Say what you want to the others, but not me. I'm done, and I mean that."

"Get up, auntie," Amelia said again, pulling her belt out of the loop of her jeans. She wrapped it around her small fist. "This is not a negotiation."

Keesh

"I swear on the grave of Lady K'abel ... if you hit me with—"

Amelia swung the belt with a ferocious scream, but her auntie caught the end and yanked it, pulling Amelia off of her feet. Amelia fell face first into the dirt. Marissa stood up holding the belt now. She smacked her niece with it on her ass and she shrieked in pain.

"This is my soil!" Marissa shouted, whipping the teen again on the behind. "I'm taking it back from you and your lunatic father!"

"No, you will not."

Marissa suddenly turned and saw her brother standing behind her. "I will not let this continue," she said to him.

"You have no choice." Vincente looked down at his daughter. "Get up. Now."

Amelia stood up. Her long silky black hair had gotten dirty.

Vincente handed her his single-action 9mm. "Your auntie has chosen to be a discontent that could possibly affect the morale of the rest of your troops. What do you do?"

Amelia lifted the handgun to Marissa's head.

"I never would have thought I would see this day," Marissa said. "Amelia, I raised you."

Villagers had stopped working. They were watching the stand-off between niece and auntie with wearisome faces.

80

Real Bitches
Do Real Things 2

"You will do as I say," Amelia stated. "Finish your job."

"No," Marissa said.

BANG!

Amelia shot her in the face, and the body fell at her feet. She looked around at all the villagers who were frozen from what they had seen. She fired two more shots in the air to galvanize them.

"Everybody get back to work!"

As told, everyone began to tool the land as if nothing just happened.

General Vincente smiled. "Nicely done, my queen. Nicely done ..."

CHAPTER 9

California Hospital Medical Center,
Los Angeles, California (Present Day)

"The Queen shot her own auntie in the face?" asked Detective Figg.

"That's how the story goes," Hershey said.

"How did they get their dope into America?"

"The General had connections from his time in the service. He invited a CIA agent to come down and check out his thriving coca plantation. They ended up working out a deal to transfer kilos out of Honduras and into the United States. The Queen joined the CIA agent on the first few trafficking trips to learn the ins and outs and also to make sure the agent held up his end of the bargain financially."

Figg looked at his watch. He had sent Neeta's interrogation video to a specialist that was skilled in detecting lies from body language and voice timbres, and in another hour the specialist should be calling to tell him what he had determined.

Figg would do the same with Hershey's recording.

"I take it the relationship between The General and the CIA agent went well," Figg said.

"Very well. But the main relationship was between the CIA agent and The Queen. They became romantically involved."

"Lovers?"

"Yep. Rumor is they ended up getting married too."

"Kids?"

"I don't think they made it that far. I don't even know if it was a real marriage. The Queen murdered the CIA agent after she didn't need him anymore. She stabbed him to death during sex."

"So The Queen killed her own auntie and her own husband for the advancement of her father's cocaine business into the U.S.?"

"Cold-hearted bitch, ain't she? That's why I'm never getting married."

"Speaking of marriages," Figg said, "I haven't had time to find out for sure if Kamau and Neeta are legally married. Do you think they are?"

"I was at the wedding."

"Were you one of the ones who signed their wedding certificate?"

"No."

"Who do I need to ask about that?"

"Vida Benitez."

Figg frowned. "Neeta said Vida wasn't invited ... well, Neeta was speaking as Vida when she said that she—or, uh, Vida—" Figg stopped, because he was confusing himself. "If Vida was at the wedding, why would Neeta say she wasn't?"

"Neeta was acting as Vida when she told you that. Neeta wanted you to believe that Vida had justification for turning on Neeta. Neeta portrayed herself as Vida—the loyal friend done wrong by her boss/friend so you'd sympathize with 'Vida'—and if you sympathized with her then that increased the chances that you'd believe Neeta was Vida during your interrogation. Follow?"

"Yes."

"Neeta fooled you good. I told you she's intelligent. She graduated Georgia State with that magna cum laude shit. In all actuality, Vida had no reason to turn on Neeta other than greed and jealousy. Neeta was good to her always. She made Vida her Maid of Honor. So you can imagine how hurt Neeta was when she found out Vida was plotting with Eddy Galvan to take over her and Kamau's operation."

"Neeta was hurt enough to blow Vida up in a car explosion."

"Exactly."

Keesh

Figg looked at his tape recorder. There wasn't much left on this side before he would have to flip it over. "You have no idea where Neeta is right now?"

"Nope. She could be anywhere in the world."

"Like Honduras?"

Hershey shrugged. "I know I said Neeta was smart, but she's also crazy. And when you mix smart and crazy the outcome can never be guessed. Neeta and Kamau could very well be down in South America chasing a coca plantation that may or may not exist. I have no idea. They don't fuck wit' me no more. I'm dead to them."

CHAPTER 10

Western Honduras
The Village

Kamau and I convinced the villagers that they needed to take back their land from Israel Trevino and the dictator he worked for. Kamau was firm with his speech, pointing out how populated this land was and that there was strength in numbers. On my turn to talk, I reminded them of their heroic Mayan ancestry and laid out a detailed plan to seize the plantation, which involved, in my own frank words, "a shitload of bravery and zero compromise." Penang translated for us, but most of the villagers already understood English pretty well. Kamau showed everyone our truck bed piled full of old but operative assault rifles that we bought on the black market from the northerners in San Pedro Sula. We both gave men, women, and boys—and two very persistent little girls—lessons on how to use the weapons.

Keesh

After weeks of preparations, one of the elders found me by the lake alone. I was on my knees, scooping my hands in the water to wash my face.

"Will you enslave us to the drug trade as well?" he asked me.

I stood up, wiping my hands dry on my jeans. The old man was shorter than me, thinner too, but his eyes looked just as alert and youthful as my own. I couldn't bullshit this man.

"No, it'll be more like a partnership," I answered him. "You guys grow it, we sell it, and the majority of the profits will remain in the village."

He stepped toward me on his cane. "What promise do we have?"

"All I have is me and my husband's word. And I'm sure you can tell that we mean well."

The old man reached into his handmade pouch and pulled out a photograph. He handed it to me, and I looked at it curiously. It was a tattered picture of a beautiful young Honduran girl. A pre-teen. She looked sad in the image.

"Who is this?" I asked.

"That is my granddaughter. Her name is Sharia. She was taken away from this village by marauders a few years ago. She is being held against her will in the governor's mansion in Santa Rosa de Copán. Please bring her back to us."

Real Bitches
Do Real Things 2

I took another look at the picture, then stuffed it in my pocket. I held out my hand, agreeing to help him. "If I find her, I'll bring her back. You have my word."

The old man shook my hand firmly, then gently pulled me into a hug.

***

I was using a D-handle fork made of forged steel to aerate the soil. And I was dressed like the rest of the villagers so I would blend in. A long dress that stopped at the ankles made of brown thread covered my frame. I had on sturdy sandals, and there was an ornamental yellow flower pinned to my updo—Trevino nor any of the foremen had recognized me.

"*¡Más rápido!*" one of the foremen shouted at an elderly woman whom I had come to know as Morella. The foreman's name was Ferdinand, and he was a stout fellow who wore a cowboy hat and a plaid shirt unbuttoned at his chest and his sleeves.

I watched as Ferdinand snatched the spade from her and stuck it in the dirt as a demonstration. He was a strong man so it went in deep, and when he shoveled out the dirt there was a large hole that would've taken Morella three times to make.

"That's how you do it," Ferdinand said.

"I'm tired," Morella moaned.

"I don't care. You work. And you work harder."

"Water, please."

"You want water?"

"Yes, sir. I'm very fatigued."

Ferdinand spit in her face. "Drink up," he laughed. "Now get back to work!"

I'd seen enough. The time was now.

Throwing down my steel fork, I stalked over to Ferdinand who had his back to me. In just a few strides I had reached under my long dress and grabbed a different kind of steel—a .38-caliber revolver. I put it to the back of his head and thumbed the hammer spur.

Click.

Ferdinand froze.

"Turn around," I said.

He did, slowly. Then he looked at me with malicious black eyes that narrowed as he tried to recognize me.

I said, "Yes, I'm the new girl. And I don't like how things are run around here."

"I suggest you put that gun down, *pinche puta*." He glanced up at the hills to the east as if I should take a look as well. I didn't. "Or you won't live to see tomorrow."

"Your sniper is dead," I said.

He looked shocked.

"Penang slit his throat. He's pretty good with a blade. And you should know because he told me you once forced him to cut down stalks with a dull pocketknife."

Ferdinand swallowed. "What do you want?"

"I want this land back in the hands of the villagers. There's a new deal that's going to take place that doesn't involve slavery. Me and my husband will be doing the cocaine distribution from here on out."

"You must have no idea what you're getting into. Israel Trevino will tell the governor and he will crush you."

"I don't think so." I looked at Morella. "Would you like to do the honors?"

"*Si,*" the old woman said eagerly.

I expected her to take my revolver from me but she didn't. She picked up the spade she had been digging with all morning.

"What is she about to do?" Ferdinand asked me with tremors in his voice, as Morella cocked the spade back like a baseball bat behind him.

"You don't wanna know," I said.

Morella swung the spade and it collided with Ferdinand's head with an audible *dong*. He hit the dirt sideways. I thought she was done, but then she stood over him and gripped the spade's handle with two hands. She brought it up and swiftly stabbed into his head with strength I didn't know she had. Ferdinand's head split in two like a watermelon, but was still partly attached by leathery strings of flesh. There was cranial blood all over the dirt, and some splashed on me and Morella's toes.

"No, *that's* how you do it," Morella said in a mocking Spanish accent, as she spat on her ex-foreman's severed face.

***

Israel Trevino should have gotten an update from his foremen by now. He swung his boots off of his desk, sat up straight in his chair and grabbed his walkie-talkie.

He pressed the PTT switch and said, "*Informe de situación,* Ferdinand."

Nobody answered him.

He took a swig from his whiskey bottle, then tried again. "*Informe de situación,* Ferdinand."

Silence. Irritating silence.

Trevino stood up from his desk and went to the window. He looked to the East at the densely vegetated hills where his sniper was supposed to be hiding. "*Informe de situación,* Sylvester!"

Trevino listened to the quiet static of his walkie-talkie and got angrier by the second. Grunting, he snatched the binoculars off of the wall peg they were hanging from, then stormed outside into the cool Honduran winds. It was always breezy up here on high ground. Sometimes the wind would take your hat clean off of your head.

As the wind whistled and ruffled his tan shirt, he peered through the binoculars and could see the plantation as if he was standing right there in the middle of the stalks. He scanned the rows, then stopped when he saw the crowd of villagers raising their tools in the air in triumph. Laying dead in the dirt in the middle of their celebratory circle was his foreman Ferdinand, his face a gory mush. His blood had soaked into the dirt and looked as black as oil.

Trevino cursed in Spanish, let the binoculars hang around his neck, then pulled out his cellphone to call the governor.

"Not so fast, compadre."

Trevino turned to see the Negro man with ponytailed dreads pointing a handgun in his face. Trevino said, "You won't make it out of Honduras alive."

"Speak for yourself."

Bang!

CHAPTER 11

California Hospital Medical Center
Los Angeles, California (Present Day)

The tape recorder stopped. Detective Figg took the tape out, turned it over and popped it back in.

He hit record.

"True or False," he said to Hershey. "Did Kamau and Neeta meet in college?"

"False. Kamau met Neeta the night he killed her brother. But they didn't officially become a couple until they got to Georgia State."

"So they just happened to end up at the same college?"

"Nah, Kamau followed her." Hershey reached behind him and readjusted his pillows. He leaned back again but still didn't look comfortable. "He had a thing for Neeta. But a lot of it was guilt. Bloodguilt. He killed her brother and he felt bad about it. Murk was her protector, and since Kamau took that from Neeta, he felt like he had to replace it by being her new protector. Everybody deals with guilt in their own way. And Kamau's way was to stalk and eventually fuck his victim's little sister."

"Neeta told me it was the other way around. She said she stalked Kamau. She kept going past the indoor pool where he swam until he noticed her."

"Kamau probably made her think she was pursuing him. I don't know how hip you are, detective, but there are ways to make a woman chase you. He probably took his shirt off when he knew she was around, showing off his little muscles and abs. That's the type of nigga he is. Ol' show-off. I bet he made himself seen, putting himself in the same room as her, learning her interests and making them his own. He was selling my dope in college, so that alone made him attractive. Whatever he did, it worked."

"So after Kamau and Neeta graduated, they teamed up and eventually moved back to California after the South got too hot for them. How did you feel about their relationship?"

"I was happy for them. They made me money."

"Kamau never thought you would tell Neeta that he killed her brother?"

"Sure he did. That was in the back of his mind. But that wasn't the reason he shot me and got me holed up in this hospital room."

"What was his reason?"

"Jealousy," Hershey said.

Figg was confused. "Jealous of what? Money?"

"No. He was jealous of Neeta."

"Why would he be jealous of her? They were a couple."

Hershey smiled. "That don't mean shit. I took Neeta's virginity."

Figg leaned back in his chair. He was starting to make sense of it all now.

"I made Neeta into the freak she is today," Hershey continued. "I was fucking her way before Kamau even knew she existed. So when they came back to Cali, he got a reminder of how close me and Neeta were. She still kicked it wit' me while they were together. We didn't fuck, but we'd still go out to eat and that burned Kamau up."

"There's something that still isn't adding up to me. If Kamau shot you, why did we find the bodies of Eddy's Honduran men in front of your dope house?"

"Because they were there too when Kamau shot me. So was Vida. He shot *everybody*. In my room me and Vida were privately discussing our way of going about this Western Honduran thing when Kamau busted in."

"Is that where you normally hold meetings? In your room?"

"Meetings with women, yes." Hershey grinned.

"You were having sex with Vida too?"

Keesh

"As soon as Neeta brought her to the team I started fucking her. I had never fucked a Honduran girl until then. I've had plenty of Mexicans, but not Honduran. Vida was a wonderful fuck." Hershey kissed his fingers in a gesture of fine taste. "She was magnificent. Had to be her stripper background that groomed her in the art of sex. She turned me out, and that doesn't happen often. I'm usually the one showing bitches new shit."

"I just wanna know what was said between you and Kamau before he shot you."

"I'm getting there. But Vida was part of that conversation, so let me put everything in perspective for you ..."

CHAPTER 12

Los Angeles, California

West 101st Street (Two weeks ago)

"You must be half ape," Hershey moaned.

He was in his bed laying on his back buck-naked, as Vida Benitez straddled him, backwards. All Hershey could see was her long Spanish hair flowing down her spine—and the bones in her spine stuck out because her back was arched. Not sexy at all. But the way she jockeyed her bare feet around his black dick was beyond sexy; it was ethereal!

"Those are hands," Hershey said, calling foul. "Those have to be hands."

"Nope," Vida said, looking back at him with a smile. She showed him her palms and wiggled her fingers. "No hands."

"Oh my God."

Her feet kneaded his shaft in a delicate rolling motion, from her toes on across her doughy soles to the heels of her feet and back again. She then formed her feet against his meat at a different angle, a cross-action massage that allowed her to bend his stiffness slightly, naturally, careful not to rupture the cylinders within the penis.

Hershey was feeling so good he started to perspire. When lightheaded-ness began to weigh in, he realized he wasn't breathing and quickly gasped, then sniffed in a big gulp of pungent pussy-scented air that ignited colorful fireworks in his mind.

Tiny rainbows of light twinkled before his eyes, and he wasn't sure if it was just her back sweat glistening or if he was merely imagining it.

"You're a beast!" Hershey exclaimed.

Playfully, Vida made a monkey call. "Ooh-ooh-ooh-ah-ah-AH!"

Hershey skeeted, couldn't help it. His cum shot out so fast it made a *tsss* sound, but it didn't spray up—it sprayed *down* because Vida had been pressing her big toe into his penis slit. She tried to trap the pleasure, and it made for an interesting tickling sensation that lingered in his testicles.

Even his stomach started to feel fluttery.

"Never have I ever ..." Hershey began, as he tried to regain his breathing. "... felt so helpless. Bravo, Vida. Brah-fucking-voe."

Vida laid down beside him and fondled his chest hairs. "I told you I could make you cum this time without pussy, hands, or mouth. That's how I was so successful at stripping. I do what other bitches are too scared to try."

"And now you're bringing that same gutter shit to the dope game. I dig it. What you and Eddy are trying to do in Honduras is big."

"But you're down, right?"

"Yeah, I'm in ... if the numbers turn out to be the same as yall say they are. I'm all about making more money."

She smiled at Hershey.

For over a decade, the Crenshaw Mafia had been receiving their cocaine from a supplier in Nevada. That's how it had always been. And within that time frame the Mafia had been approached with better cocaine deals than that Nevada plug—*very* competitive prices per kilo and broader distribution—but Murk's dumb ass had always turned those deals down because he was quote/unquote "loyal" to his Nevada connection. Hershey, on the other hand, saw loyalty as a mental roadblock. Loyalty meant nothing nowadays; it was a quality that was cool to stick to as long as it made sense financially.

This deal with Vida and Eddy would be Hershey's first opportunity since he'd become leader of the Crenshaw Mafia. And he was going to take it.

"Don't forget about our stipulation though," Vida warned him. "No supplying Neeta and Kamau."

"You really hate her, huh?" Hershey asked.

"Yeah. She thinks she's hot shit. Always rubbing what she has in my face. Now she's gonna know who the real boss bitch is. I'll be the plug, not the runner. I'll own a whole cocaine plantation. And when me and Eddy get married, our relationship will be ten times better than Kamau and Neeta's."

"I admit, Neeta has damn sure gotten a big head. She's like my little sister, but she needs to be brought back down to reality. She's not the boss. And when she starts starving she'll realize that."

"No serving her, Hershey. Even when she starts starving, don't help her."

Hershey looked over at Vida, eyeing her sexy, slender curves up and down. In one breath she had talked of marrying Eddy, but just a few moments ago her feet had been coddling his dick. He admired Vida and her selfish premeditated plans to reach the top. He never met a woman like her before. She reminded him of himself.

Firmly, she seized his jaw in one hand. "Did you hear me?"

"Yes, baby."

"If I find out you gave Neeta my bricks, I'll cut you off. And then you'll have to go back to the shitty plug with the overpriced mediocre dope you've been using." She let his face go, then smiled again. "So how does it feel buying your dope from a woman?"

"I'm fine with it. I already tell people my dope comes from The Queen."

"Now you'll be telling the truth."

"You're more arrogant than Neeta."

Vida laughed, then gave him a juicy kiss. Hershey moved into the kiss, rolling on top of her. He was about to stick his dick between her legs when someone knocked on the door.

"Who is it?" Hershey said over his shoulder. He thought it was Eddy's men, who were supposed to be waiting in the kitchen. They were under the impression that Hershey and Vida were just in here having a meeting.

"It's Kamau."

Hershey said, "What the fuck do you want? I'm in a meeting."

"It's about Neeta."

"What about her?"

"You already know what."

A defensive tone. Hershey heard it in the man's voice. "Hold on, nigga," he said, as he crawled off of Vida. First thing he did was strap on his bulletproof vest before slipping into the rest of his clothes. Vida started putting on her panties, and she watched him as he tucked his gun in his waist.

"What does he want?" Vida whispered.

"To tell me to leave Neeta alone."

"You're fucking her too?"

"No."

Hershey opened the door, and Kamau was standing there with the hard expression of a man who wanted to seem intimidating. Hershey walked past him to the kitchen, where the Honduran henchman in tailored suits sat at the table patiently. Hershey put on a chef hat and apron, and started stirring the cake batter he'd started before company arrived.

"I need to talk to you," Kamau said, appearing in the kitchen a second later.

"Talk." Hershey kept stirring.

"I don't wanna talk in front of them."

The Honduran men were observant, but also respectfully quiet.

"They don't even know English," Hershey said.

Vida walked in the kitchen next. She had her shirt buttoned and her hair combed, and her stretchy chic skirt was glued to her legs in fashion excellence, as if it hadn't just been laying on Hershey's floor a minute ago. She patted Kamau on the back as she went and stood behind her escorts seated at the kitchen table. She put a hand on each of her men's shoulders and they stood up beside her.

"Hi, Kamau," said Vida. "Sorry to leave as soon as you came."

"Why are you here?" Kamau asked her rudely.

"I'm getting some more dope from Hershey so I can make you and your wife more millions."

"Get moving then."

"Oh, I am. In due time I'll be moving faster than you thought possible."

"What's that supposed to mean?"

"Inside joke."

Vida winked at Hershey, who hid his smile by lifting his spatula to his lips and licking the batter. Vida left with the two Honduran men.

"We're alone now," Hershey said. "Tell me what's on your mind."

"Stay away from Neeta," Kamau said.

"I haven't fucked her since she was a teenager."

"I don't care. I don't want yall going out together no more."

"Tell your wife that, not me."

Kamau pulled his gun out and pointed it at Hershey's head. "I said leave her alone. I'm serious, Hershey. Respect my wishes."

"Respect goes both ways. I've respected yall's relationship. But this right here, you putting a gun in my face, ain't respect. And if you're counting on me not to be around Neeta at all, you got another thing coming. She gets dope from me. The both of yall do. And I think that's been forgotten. *I run this shit*. And even before this dope shit, Neeta's been like my baby sister. I have to look out for her, especially when she's in LA."

"That's *my* job now."

"You really think that job only belongs to you? Kamau, you'd be stupid to shoot me. It'll be suicide. Our Crenshaw brothers are hanging out outside on the steps right now. Do you think they're gonna let you walk away from this house when they hear the shot? Of course not. Don't be silly, Kamau. Get that gun outta my face."

They both turned their heads when they saw Vida and one of the Honduran bodyguards walk back in the kitchen.

"I almost forgot what I came to—" Vida suddenly froze before she reached the duffel bag of dope she'd left sitting on the counter. She looked shocked to see Kamau holding a gun to Hershey's head. "Am I interrupting something?"

Hershey licked his spatula once more, then stuck it back in the bowl. "Kamau, go home. This is the second time you've made me regret my decision to bring you into the Mafia."

"The Crenshaw Mafia wouldn't be shit without me and Neeta."

Vida butted in. "So what am I? Chopped liver?"

Hershey waved his palm at her. "Chill, Vida. Let me talk to him."

"No, Hershey. You heard how he just talked to you. You're the leader of the Crenshaw Mafia, not him. And not

Neeta. If I was you I would cut their ass off right now. I know all their clientele personally so I'll move your dope without them until me and Eddy's dope comes through. Cut his ass off now, Hershey."

"I said chill, Vida."

"Fuck that! Tell his high and mighty ass he's done!"

"Yall been planning to cut me and my wife out?" Kamau asked Hershey, still holding the gun in his face.

Hershey sighed. He didn't want to do it this way. "I think it might be time for me to cut you and Neeta loose. Yall have gotten too bigheaded for the Mafia."

"There has to be a meeting. You can't just cut us off."

"Well, we will finish this at the meeting. But the rest of the CMG brothers will rule in my favor. Nobody likes what you and Neeta have become. You guys think you're celebrities."

Kamau lowered his gun and snorted. "Me and Neeta bring the most money in. We'll see who gets voted out." Kamau scowled at Vida. "You think you can take our clientele? Yeah right. I wish Neeta would've never hired you. I knew you was a snake. You won't make it that much longer in this business. You're on my list."

"Me cago en ti," Vida cursed. *"Yo soy la reina!"*

"Right back at you, bitch." Kamau started out of the kitchen, then said over his shoulder, "Stay away from my wife, Hershey. No more warnings."

Keesh

"If I wanted to fuck your wife again, I could," Hershey said, and Kamau stopped in his tracks, turned and threw a warning glare. But Hershey antagonized him more. "I can't help how she feels about me. When you're somebody's first, you always hold that special place in their heart."

Kamau lifted his gun in anger and fired.

CHAPTER 13

California Hospital Medical Center
Los Angeles, California (Present Day)

"I knew he was sensitive about his woman," Hershey said to Detective Figg, "but I didn't think he was sensitive enough to shoot me in my own house while I was baking a cake for my daughter. Remind me to never joke about a man's wife again."

Detective Figg was leaning back in his seat with his legs crossed. As he stared at Hershey, his head was tilted on his hand in a contemplative way. He wasn't sure if he believed what Hershey just told him. The whole sex story with Vida and her fancy feet could have been completely fabricated. Men lied about who they've slept with all the time. Figg had lied a time or two in his younger days, and at the precinct his male coworkers told sex lies over coffee almost every morning. And from what Figg had learned through investigation and witness interviews, Kamau didn't seem like a jealous person. Surely not jealous enough to shoot another man for merely being around his wife. There had to be another reason Kamau shot Hershey—*if* he even pulled the trigger at all.

Figg made sure to cast his voice with skepticism. "Neeta told me one of Eddy's henchman shot you. She said Vida was trying to rob you and it went wrong."

"If you believe Neeta's story, what the fuck you asking me for then?"

"I'm not saying I believe her. I wanna know why she would tell me that."

"Simple. She didn't want Kamau to face the charges. She blamed it on Vida, the dead girl."

"There was a lot that happened after you got shot. More shots were fired, one of the henchmen was killed, and the other henchman escaped through the garage with Vida, but he was gunned down and he hit a fire hydrant. Vida was taken and later killed. Forensics match that account. What pieces can you add to that?"

"Nothing. I was laying on the floor bleeding to death. Anything after I got shot I can't help you with."

"But your Crenshaw brothers surely know. They were there hanging around 101st Street, right?"

"After I got shot, I heard Kamau went on a shooting spree. I heard the Mafia helped him capture Vida, because they didn't know Kamau was the one that shot me. One of my lieutenants told me that Kamau was hollering, *'Get Vida, get Vida!'* They thought Vida and Eddy's guys shot me. They took Vida to the Bellevue Recreation Center where Neeta forced her to tell her about our plans to cross her and Kamau out. I heard most of the Crenshaw Mafia was there backing them up. Kamau and Neeta tricked the Mafia. They didn't know Kamau was really the one that hit their boss."

"What else did you hear happened at Bellevue?"

Hershey gave a smile. "Neeta challenged Vida to a basketball game. That shit is funny as fuck."

"How so?"

"Because I taught her how to play."

"Her brother Murk didn't teach her?"

"He probably taught her how to dribble, how to put the ball in the hoop, but I taught her how to *ball*. I'm the genius behind everything Neeta does today, and that's why Kamau shot me. I taught her how to cook dope the right way. I even taught her how to fuck."

"How old was Neeta when you took her virginity?"

"I've been waiting for you to ask that question. I can tell you didn't want to ask it."

"How old, Hershey?"

"Fifteen."

Detective Figg shook his head disappointedly. "You were twenty-five at the time. That's a serious crime."

Keesh

"So is stealing Cable."

"You said you were the genius who molded her. What was she like growing up? Had she always leaned toward crime?"

"No. She liked books and reading and learning new things. Everybody around her was living a life of crime and she tried to steer us away from it. When she was real little, she gave us all jobs at her lemonade stand and said we could stop committing felonies."

"What changed?"

"Reality hit. In her teen years she started seeing how the real world works. She wanted money. She wanted popularity. She wanted to be remembered for something, good or bad, like the people she used to read about in those books. She already knew how to be bad from us, so that's what she chose."

"What makes her tick?"

"Two things—fame and fucking. Sounds harsh, but that pretty much sums her up. Let me explain to you what I mean ..."

CHAPTER 14

Crenshaw High School
2003

Fifteen-year-old Neeta Lockett threw her backpack on the floor of the seat, then hopped in on the passenger side. She smacked the dash of the Mercedes-Benz twice. "Let's go! Let's get a move on! Hit it, Brittany!"

Her driver, Brittany Jolston, gave her a playful side-eye. "Girl, I'ma get you to yo audition on time. Settle down."

"I don't want to be late. I really think I can get this part."

"I do too. And so does Hershey. Do you have your script?"

"Shit, I left it in my locker."

"Run back in there and get it."

Neeta looked out her window at the front of Crenshaw High. Students were still piling out in droves, bumping each other and running into the parking lot at offbeat speeds. It would be a pain fighting that traffic.

"Fuck it, Brittany. I rehearsed enough. I know my lines by heart. Let's get out of here before the buses start pulling out."

"You sure?"

"Hit it, bitch!"

Brittany laughed, then mashed her foot down on the gas pedal, causing Neeta to slam back against her seat. The white Mercedes-Benz shot through the school parking lot, Brittany wheeling it expertly around students too slow to get out of her way.

Brittany Jolston was a getaway driver, or used to be when she first joined the Crenshaw Mafia. Now she was Hershey's on-again/off-again girlfriend and Neeta's personal driver. It had been weird for Neeta, at first, hanging out with Brittany because Neeta had a crush on Hershey. But Brittany, being the strong and confident woman she was, thought the crush on her man was cute and didn't feel threatened at all.

"A lot of girls like Hershey," Brittany told her once. "I don't care. I only got one rule—if you wanna fuck him, you have to fuck me first."

Neeta had laughed when she said it, thought Brittany was joking. But she later learned that Brittany went both ways.

Today, Brittany was taking her to a callback audition in Burbank, off West Alameda Avenue. This would be audition number thirty-six, and callback number one. So Neeta was anxious.

They got caught by a red light and she cursed.

"Calm down," Brittany said. "Getting all worked up won't help you."

"This is my first callback. I don't wanna be late."

"You won't. I'm behind the wheel. What are you auditioning for?"

"The role of a fraud investigator's daughter. The investigator digs a little too deep into the wrong company and his daughter gets kidnapped. The daughter's boyfriend—that the investigator father hates—happens to be with her and he gets snatched too. They plot their escape together. It's action-based, but there's comedy in it too."

"That sounds like a good movie."

"I know. This could jumpstart my career."

"Why do you wanna be an actress?"

Neeta smiled. "The money and fame."

"Which one do you want more?"

"The money!"

Brittany laughed and gave her a high-five.

But deep down all Neeta really wanted was the fame, to have her face on the big screen with moviegoers gawking at her beauty. She already had money—well, her big brother Murk did as leader of the Crenshaw Mafia—so she was used to spending as she pleased. She'd even experienced a little bit of fame from being popular at school. And even that little bit was addictive. But being an actress was the *ultimate* popularity, the quintessential stamp of worldwide notoriety.

They made it to the audition on time. Early, actually. Neeta and Brittany got to sit in the nearly-empty auditorium a few rows back from the producers and casting agents and watch another girl and guy perform the same escape scene Neeta would have to. Together, they stared in amazement at the talented couple and the mesmerizing kiss at the end. The producers and casting agents gave them a standing ovation, and Neeta and Brittany clapped too.

"You have to kiss somebody?" Brittany asked Neeta.

"Yep."

"You think you can outdo her?"

"I think I can."

"Don't think. *Know.* You're too pretty to be lacking in confidence. Too damn pretty."

Neeta stood when her name was called, and Brittany patted her butt and told her to knock 'em dead. She approached the front of the auditorium, looking over at her male co-actor as he stepped on stage with her. His name was Dwight. He was brown-skinned with a small afro, the nerdy type. He was dressed in a brownish wool sweater that he confidently tugged up the sleeves of, just enough to show his wrists. He held his script in his hand.

Neeta's was still in her locker.

"And ... action!" one of the producers yelled.

Dwight's line was first. He grabbed Neeta's arm as part of the performance. "We have to get out of here *now*. They'll kill us if we just sit here."

Neeta replied on point. "No, my daddy will come. He'll save us."

"He's just gonna call the damn police. And you heard what they said they'll do if the police show up."

"They won't kill us."

"Yes, they will. I know they will."

"How can you be so sure?"

Dwight drew closer to her, creating suspense. "Because my dad is one of the kidnappers."

Neeta and Dwight nailed their lines. Then came the kiss—the scripted kiss that Dwight forced upon Neeta to convince her to join him in escape. When his lips pushed against hers, it was her job to pretend to be enveloped by it. She tried to imagine she was kissing Hershey, but it didn't work. Dwight's mouth was nasty—not in smell but in excessive saliva—and Neeta felt her insides clinch in reaction to the repulsive kiss and she pulled away from him, which wasn't in the script.

Keesh

***

"She didn't get the part," Brittany said to Hershey, who was in his kitchen on West 101st Street cooking dope on the stove. "Neeta memorized her lines good, but she tanked on the kissing part and that killed the whole thing."

Hershey was gripping the top of a jar, swirling the liquid pre-freebase round and round. "Where is she?"

"In the front room sitting on the couch."

"Why'd you bring her here?"

"Because she didn't want to go home yet and tell her brother she failed," Brittany said, planting her hands on her hips. "And I told her I would teach her how to kiss."

Hershey stopped swirling the jar. His interest was piqued. "How are you gonna do that?"

Brittany gave him a look, as she shifted her weight to the other foot. She waved her finger back and forth between him and herself in a "me and you" gesture. "We're gonna show her how it's done," she said, smiling.

Hershey stared at her for a moment. He knew what Brittany was suggesting. This wasn't the first time she brought a girl home for them to share. But with Neeta—who was not only underage but the boss's little sister—this time Brittany could be pushing it.

"Please," Brittany whispered, clasping all ten fingers together in a single, pleading fist. She shook the fist for emphasis. "Please, baby."

Hershey took his apron off and threw it on the counter. "Neeta, come in here!"

In a few seconds Neeta was standing in the kitchen with them. She crossed her arms and leaned against the wall, and she didn't make eye contact with Hershey because she was obviously disappointed in herself.

Brittany put her arm around her. "I told her she needs real life experiences to draw from when acting. And if she doesn't know how to be sexual, she might as well hang up her acting career."

"You wanna learn how to kiss?" Hershey asked her.

Neeta nodded.

"Look at me."

Neeta looked up.

"Do you wanna learn how to kiss?" Hershey asked her again.

"Yes, nigga," she said.

"Does Murk know you're here?"

"No."

"And he won't ever know you were here, right?"

"Right."

Hershey had to have his bases covered, had to make sure what happened here today ended up on the hush-hush list. Because if Murk found out that his little sister was here getting kissing lessons he'd be ready to murder somebody.

Keesh

Hershey opened up the refrigerator and grabbed a bottle of premium vodka. He held it out to Neeta. "Drink this. Drink it straight. And then we can get started."

Neeta took the bottle and started reading the alcohol content label, so Brittany snatched it from her and poured the girl a shot. She made Neeta drink it in one gulp. Neeta doubled over and started coughing.

"Good girl," Brittany said, patting her on the back.

Hershey led the way to his room, had a seat on his bed and Brittany joined him. Neeta paused halfway inside the room, until Brittany gave her the "come here" finger and she sat down with them, folding one leg under her and leaning back on her hands in an effort to get comfortable. Hershey could tell she wasn't though. Her eyes said it all.

She's gonna change her mind, Hershey thought. *She's not gonna want to go through with this.*

Still, he started his demonstration on Brittany with a single-lip kiss.

"Pay attention," Brittany said, as she pulled away. "Watch how we take turns leading with our lips. Let him lead first, learn his rhythm, learn whether he favors your top or bottom lip, give him tongue—not too much—and always start off leaning to the right. Always. Got it?"

Neeta nodded. "Mmm-hmm. I got it."

Hershey and Brittany dived back in, and the passion began to build. Hershey sucked on her slithery pink tongue with his eyes closed, but he lifted his lids and peeked through slits when he felt Brittany again begin to back off a little. Reason why: she was reaching out and grabbing Neeta by the neck, and she tenderly pulled her face into the fold. Brittany was being greedy.

"Don't be shy," Brittany said to Neeta, kissing her softly. "We're gonna make you a star."

Hershey was surprised that Neeta didn't run out of the room in fear, which one girl Brittany brought home had done before. Instead, Neeta kissed Brittany back with the patience of a dutiful student, and Hershey genuinely started to feel like he was doing a good thing. But when Brittany guided Neeta's mouth to his and their lips meshed, Neeta started to get more excited than she should have—she grabbed his hand sensually, squeezed it—and to Hershey it quickly felt less and less like training and more like seduction. Neeta's breathing got faster, and her lips began to apply a growing forward pressure as if kissing was a game of who-pushes-hardest. Neeta was clearly turned on by male stimulation. Hershey grabbed her face, made her stop.

She let out a tiny lustful moan, puckering her lips for more. Her eyes were still closed.

"Doing good," Brittany urged, smiling. "Lose yourself, Neeta. Show him what you got. Hershey, let her go. Let her practice."

Keesh

Hershey had a moment of regret, but he was never one to turn down a good time so he pulled Neeta down on the bed, got on top of her and tore her shirt open. He was kissing her harder, biting flesh, kissing on her prominent chin, which led to undressing, which led to passionate groping between their many hands, and somehow Brittany ended up right where she couldn't wait to be—between his legs bogarting to eat Neeta's pussy. Hershey thought it was too soon, that maybe he should have warmed Neeta up with oral first.

But Neeta surprised him.

"Fuck me good after she's done," Neeta said to him hoarsely. "I want my first dick to be yours."

At that point Hershey knew Neeta would never be the same.

CHAPTER 15

California Hospital Medical Center
Los Angeles, California (Present Day)

"Me and Brittany created a sexual monster that day," Hershey said as if he wasn't proud of what he'd done. He was staring off into space, still caught in the memory. "I thought I was helping her. Really, I did think of it as help. But she didn't go to one audition after that. She just wanted to hang around me and Brittany."

Detective Figg excused himself to go use the johnny, the guest stall inside the room. As he stood over the toilet unzipping and then relieving himself, he thought about Neeta Bryant laying underneath Hershey and Brittany receiving extraordinary pleasure. The imagery Figg started conjuring up in his mind was giving him a woody, making it difficult for him to pee in the bowl. He had to take a couple steps back and aim low.

Keesh

And this was a strange thing, Figg being turned on by a suspect. He'd went after plenty of female criminals throughout his career in law enforcement, some drop-dead gorgeous, and he'd never felt attracted to any of them. Not one. But Neeta was a different kind of beauty. She had intelligence to back up the physical, she outsmarted him so cleverly, *brilliantly*, and Figg had always loved a smart woman. Maybe he was a sapiosexual and didn't know it. But even with his inappropriate desire to sleep with Neeta, he was still going to capture her and throw her behind bars for the rest of her life.

Figg shook his peter until it shrunk enough for him to stuff it back in his pants and zip up. Then he flushed the toilet and washed his hands, staring at himself in the mirror.

"Stay focused, detective," he said to himself.

When he walked out, Hershey was setting his cell phone back down on the medical overbed table.

"Who were you talking to?" Figg asked.

"Nobody. I was just looking at the internet."

Figg sat back down and noticed his recorder had stopped. "Did you touch this?"

"Yeah. It was recording nothing. I was saving you space on the tape."

"Don't ever touch my recorder."

"Okay."

Figg started the tape. "How many times did you sleep with Neeta after that?"

"Gah-lee, uh ... I don't know, maybe fifty times. She got tired of Brittany being involved after the third time. All she wanted was dick. Morning, noon, and night."

"And you never slept with her after she started seeing Kamau?"

"No. I'm not like that."

"But Kamau shot you anyway."

"Yeah. Ego shit. But like I told you, it was me blurting out that I could still fuck Neeta that made him mad. I should've kept my mouth shut."

"Let's get back to the true or false. Neeta Bryant met Vida Benitez at the strip club."

"True."

"Vida started running the drugs that Kamau and Neeta purchased from you."

"True."

"Vida and Eddy Galvan approached you with a deal to cut out Kamau and Neeta."

"True."

"Kamau shot you because of jealousy. It wasn't drug-related."

Hershey nodded. "True again."

"And about the Bellevue Recreation Center ... What did you hear happened after the basketball game between Neeta and Vida?"

"What did Neeta tell you?"

"I don't answer questions. I ask them."

Hershey said, "I heard Eddy and his people showed up to rescue Vida. But Neeta and Kamau and the Crenshaw Mafia held it down; they won the shoot-out. Eddy got away. Vida didn't. Neeta stuck that bitch in a whip and blew her ass up to fake her own death. Is that what Neeta told you? I know she did. She wouldn't be able to resist bragging about that."

Detective Figg didn't respond to him. What Hershey said about Bellevue lined up with what Neeta said, and it also matched forensics. The DA would be able to prove in court that Neeta and Kamau were drug traffickers who car-bombed a co-conspirator. Life in prison was preordained for them now.

I just have to catch them first.

A nurse walked in the room and told Hershey she needed a urine sample. So Detective Figg stood up and excused himself. He walked out of the room and down the hall to the waiting area, where he stood in front of a muted flatscreen with his hands stuffed in his pockets. He had gotten some good information from Hershey but it wasn't enough to bring back to the chief of police, Stephen Beck. Figg needed a solid lead, not speculation. His boss wouldn't accept anything less.

A newsblast popped up on the television. Fox News was flashing images of what looked like a war-torn Third

World country. Detective Figg started to turn away and have a seat, but then his eyes zeroed in on the screen when he saw "Santa Rosa de Copán, Western Honduras" scroll across the news ticker. There was a gun battle taking place behind a foreign reporter that kept repeating on a 10-second clip. The Fox anchorman was speaking on the footage of the reporter caught in the crossfire, but Figg couldn't hear a thing because there was no volume. He looked over his shoulder for a nurse with a remote, saw nobody, then he looked back at the TV and took a step toward it.

"Kamau and Neeta, is that you two?" Figg said to himself. He took his hands out of his pockets and crossed his arms, staring closely at the TV.

CHAPTER 16

Western Honduras
Santa Rosa de Copán (Present Day)

Kamau almost ran over a Santa Rosa reporter as we flew down a narrow road—and by "narrow," I really mean *super fucking tight*. One error, one slight turn of the wheel either way, and me, Kamau and Penang would crash into a parked car and none of us would survive it. But this was the only road that led to the governor's mansion. And if we slowed down then the local *policia* would have easy targets.

"There should be no parking on this street!" I yelled over the wind.

Penang was standing up in the back seat, one hand gripping the Jeep's rollover bar and his other hand holding an AK-47 cocked to the sky. I thought we were driving too fast for him to be standing up, but the skinny village boy looked calm with his weapon.

Keesh

He answered me with a yell of his own. "This is as wide as this road gets! Don't worry! Almost there!"

But I *was* worried. Kamau was trying hard to steer us down a cheap road and I was holding an FN 15 carbine shooting from the Jeep at any corrupt Santa Rosa cops with a gun. My trigger hand felt numb from the vibrations of shooting so much. My long hair blew wildly in the wind, slapping against my face and getting stuck in my mouth. I was so close to unsheathing my dagger and cutting a pile of it off.

"Freedom!" one of the villagers in the pick-up truck in front of us shouted.

Their truck had two in the cab and three in the bed, everyone armed. They were leading the way to the mansion, and I suddenly saw enormous property peek over the hills in front of us. It was magnificent, unlike anything I had ever seen in the United States. Its exterior balcony was built of pristine white stone, and the lot of land the mansion sat on was a lively green and stretched farther than the eyes could see.

The wrought iron entry gates were closed.

"How are we gonna get in?!" I shouted.

"Watch and see!" Penang said excitedly. "José, who's driving the truck in front of us, was forced to help build this fortress! Those gates won't hold!"

Real Bitches
Do Real Things 2

I put my rifle in my lap, gripping my door and the center console. The truck ahead of us plowed through the gate and I was amazed as it knocked one side completely off its hinges. I braced myself as we drove over the iron, bumpity-bumped over the bars, and we were in.

"Freedom!"

Spanish men in suits stormed out of the mansion with assault rifles. They came running out the front and also up top piling onto the balcony, shooting at us all at once. We fired back, as we made our way around to the back of the mansion. Bullets struck our Jeep and pitted the dirt near our tires but Kamau didn't stop driving and I didn't stop shooting back.

We made it to the back of the estate and parked by a luxurious kidney-shaped swimming pool. Kamau flattened a lawn chair under our wheels. Since the governor's men were all still up front, the back entrance was clear. We all jumped out with our weapons. The villagers who were in the truck smiled at us and ran under the covered patio. Me, Kamau, and Penang went the top way, up the rear staircase that boasted over fifty steps. We were winded when we reached the top, but Kamau still had the strength to ram his shoulder into the two-panel doors and bust them open.

"¡Por aquí!" a maid yelled, calling for help.

I hesitated.

Penang gunned her down.

Keesh

"I thought our villagers work here," I said, explaining the reason I hesitated to shoot.

"She from a different village," Penang said. He put his sandal foot on her chest and shot her again. "She known for getting staff beat for things she stole herself."

"Where's the governor's room?" I asked.

"Follow me," he said.

Penang had worked here in this mansion as a servant when he was eight years old. All was well until he reached his teen years and he had to serve other boys his age—ones related to the governor or other crooked politicians. They teased him or barked ridiculous orders at him. *More salt, village rat!" "Fix my tie, shine my boots, clean the shit around the toilet now!"* He told me he reached a breaking point when the governor's 10-year-old nephew smacked him across the face for placing his fork on the wrong side of the plate. Penang broke the younger boy's nose and was ultimately beaten for it and forced to work back in the coca fields.

One good thing that came out of it was he knew where to lead us now.

Somewhere below us there was gunfire, and we knew the second half of our team had encountered the enemy. I hoped we were winning, that they could at least hold them off until we murdered the governor.

Penang stopped at a door, shot the gold-plated knob with his assault rifle and kicked the door open.

"The governor is in here—!" he began.

A big shotgun blast from inside lifted him off of his feet and threw him into the wall across the hall. There was a gaping hole where his chest used to be, and an ungodly amount of blood poured out.

"Nooooo!" I screamed, and when I started to run to the boy, Kamau yanked me back by the arm and he took the lead.

He fired his assault rifle through the walls, shells kicking out everywhere, as he flew past the room. He squatted on the other side of the door, aimed inside and fired again in short bursts. I heard bodies drop. He ran in and I went in after him.

"Stop!"

The governor said it, while holding a pistol to the head of a pretty girl in a fancy shift dress with long blousine sleeves. The governor was dressed in a tailored suit. He was a middle-aged Honduran with a handsome face. With his arm around the girl's neck, he pushed the barrel further into her temple, making her head lean.

"Get out of my mansion, you rebels! I have no gold here! "

"We're not rebels and we don't want gold," Kamau said, his rifle trained on the governor.

Mines was aimed at him too but I was moving to the left. I stepped over a dead bodyguard to find a clear shot.

Keesh

The girl he was holding looked to be in her late teens, and Penang wasn't here to tell us if she was a friendly.

"If you aren't rebels, what do you want?"

"Freedom for the villagers," Kamau said.

"Done."

"That means the coca fields return to them as well."

The governor blinked, and then his gun arm suddenly went forward to shoot Kamau. I fired first. The governor and the girl went down.

Cautiously, I approached their bodies.

The girl screamed, startling me. She threw the governor's limp arm off of her and stood up, her designer dress now smeared with blood.

"You killed him!" she screamed at me. It sounded like she was angry about it.

"I saved you," I said.

"Get away from me!"

"What's your name?" Kamau asked. "What village are you from?"

"My name is Sharia and I'm not a village girl anymore."

I gasped. This was the young girl that the old man with the cane wanted me to find. I lowered my rifle and told Kamau to do the same.

"Your grandfather's been looking for you. C'mon, hurry." I grabbed her wrist, but she pulled away.

"I'm not going back to the village! I hate village life!"

Real Bitches
Do Real Things 2

"I made a promise," I told her. "You have to come."

I grabbed her again but she fought me. Kamau had to pick her up over his shoulder and carry her out. She went with us, kicking and screaming.

***

General Vincente Magana was storming down the halls of his base camp in Southern Honduras. He pulled his peak cap from under his arm and stuffed it on his head, and now he was dressed from top to bottom in full military garb.

"I want those responsible found now!" he barked at his military assistants who were tagging behind him. He turned sharply, heading down the corridor that led to the hangar, and his assistants struggled to keep pace.

"We were forwarded these pictures," said his female assistant, speeding up to hand him the photos. Her name was Fria Ramirez and she had been working side by side with The General for the last three months. "Israel Trevino sent them to us, and we've gotten word that he's been killed since then. The two people in these photos are believed to be responsible for this overthrow."

Vincente stopped abruptly, and his assistants almost bumped into him. He stared at the pictures, confused. "They're Negro."

"Yes," said Fria. "They're from America."

Keesh

The male assistant, a former soldier named Laizo Grec, added to the briefing. "From California, to be exact. I ran their faces through the system. They're names are Kamau Bryant and Neeta Bryant. They're wanted by the FBI and CIA for cocaine distribution."

"Cocaine?" The General said.

"Yes, sir," both assistants said.

Vincente then knew what they were after—his cocaine plantation, which he had entrusted the governor and the local *policia* to uphold. No one in the military high rankings knew he was connected to the plantation. If they did, he'd be dishonorably discharged for a second time.

"The two Negroes rallied men and women from villages around Santa Rosa de Copán," said Fria. "They took over the governor's mansion."

"Did they kill him?"

"We don't know yet," Laizo said.

"What do they want?" Vincente asked, even though he knew.

"They haven't sent any demands," said Fria.

General Vincente Magana walked off, moving faster than before. "We're going to Santa Rosa. Get the troops in order."

CHAPTER 17

Western Honduras
The Village (Present Day)

One thing me and Kamau knew how to do was celebrate. We danced together with the villagers around a blazing bonfire. Kamau had his shirt off and I had on a T-shirt drenched in sweat. Everything on my body that was bounceable—my hair, my breasts, a jiggle of stomach fat that snuck up on me—went out of control as I did dances these people had never seen, dances they thought were the funniest thing ever.

I was feeding off the villagers' happiness. I loved to see people smile. I had to pass on the *chicha de yuca*, which was their version of beer. I didn't want to drink. Kamau had a few sips of it from a wooden bowl. I could tell he was feeling it. He had let his dreads hang and was bouncing on his tip toes like he was at a rock concert.

Keesh

He came and held me from behind, and we swayed our hips side to side as we watched the crowd clap for a village elder who was doing some kind of high-knee shuffle in honor of Penang's lifelong bravery.

"We're doing a good thing, right?" I asked Kamau.

"No question," he said. "You're having second thoughts?"

"We came down here to take what Eddy and Vida had tried to use against us. We're here for revenge, and it feels wrong now that I've met these people."

"It's not wrong. We're here to start a pipeline of cocaine to America that'll help them more than it will us."

"But it started as revenge, Kamau. You heard what the shaman Antebella said: there's a lot of death and destruction in our future."

"You believed her?"

"She knew about Murk."

Kamau let me go and I turned around to face him. His lips were tightly pressed together, and he was giving me a look as if I was bugging out.

"We came too far to turn back now," he said. "These people are counting on us to turn their lives around and if we back out we will be doing them a disservice. That Shaman didn't know what she was talking about. She was guessing. Her stories were just about as real as The Queen and The General."

Real Bitches
Do Real Things 2

"The story of The Queen has to have some truth to it. The cocaine plantation was real."

He put his hands on my face gently. "You're the only queen I believe in. That story of The General and The Queen was just to scare people from coming down here. Eddy knew it and Vida knew it too." He kissed me, then brought his hands down to my wrists. Embers from the bonfire floated between us. "We've built something big, and it's about to get bigger. We just have to stay focused."

"But Antebella—" I began.

"Enough with that shaman lady," he said. He looked up at the sky and sighed, something he always did when he was tired of hearing me talk.

"She was telling the truth about secrets, Kamau. And if it'll keep us from the death and destruction she mentioned, I have to be honest with you right now. I've been keeping a secret from you."

He brought his chin back down quickly and stared me in the eyes. "What?"

"I think I'm pregnant."

"What the hell?! I wouldn't have brought us down here and put us in this much danger if I'd known you were carrying our child. Neeta, how could you keep that from me? We don't do that type of shit. How long have you known?"

"That's the thing. I don't know for sure. I said I *think* I'm pregnant. I didn't start thinking about it until after we talked to Antebella. I was trying to figure out the secrets she was talking about. Then I remembered when we got off the plane and I realized I was late with my period and I didn't tell you then because I wanted to be sure. It was an innocent secret."

"So you don't know if you're pregnant or not?"

"No. I won't know until I go see a doctor," I said. He looked at the sky again, but this time I knew it was just from him being overwhelmed. I waited until he looked down at me again, then I asked, "What's your secret?"

One of his eyebrows went up. "Huh?"

"Antebella said we have to get our secrets out. What's yours?"

Even though he was looking at me like I was crazy, I knew he was holding something back. I knew my husband. Even before our marriage I had always felt like there was some underlying pain in his heart that he hadn't shared with me. A few times, back in college, I had caught him sitting by himself in front of the university in deep thought. I would watch him from afar, could see his mind turning but I never asked him what had him so disturbed.

"What is it, Kamau?"

"I don't keep secrets from you," he said.

He's lying to me.

There was a sudden frightening *woosh* of flame that shot the bonfire high into the sky. Kamau held me close as we saw one of the benches catch fire and villagers scramble to put the blaze out. Then I saw Sharia, the girl we rescued from the mansion, throw another bowl of *chicha de yuca* into the fire and it *wooshed* again.

"I'm tired of this place!" Sharia screamed in a tantrum. "This shitty beer and all these damn flies! I want TELEVISION!"

The old man who asked me to bring Sharia back approached her on his cane. "Sharia, this is your home. We've missed you, you were freed from your captors, and we're celebrating your return."

"I was free in the mansion," she snapped at him. "I was living fine there until those fuckers right there showed up." She pointed at me and Kamau, then said, "Grandpa, I'm going back to Santa Rosa de Copán. I'm not a village girl anymore. I want my designer clothes, I want my nails done. I wanna go to real parties with real music. This is fuckin' bullshit!"

"Sharia," the old man said sadly, taking a precarious cane-step closer so he could touch her arm. "You always loved the village when you were a little—"

Sharia shoved her grandpa aside and he fell on his butt, and she raced across the grass toward the flatbed 4x4. I started to go after her but Kamau grabbed my arm.

"We need to talk," he said to me. "Is your head here? Do you wanna continue on our mission?"

141

Keesh

"Yes. I still wanna take over the world with you. I just had a moment of doubt."

"I need you to be one hundred percent on this, Neeta."

"Okay, but let me get Sharia first and talk some sense into her," I said.

We saw Sharia hop in the first truck she saw, and after a moment inside the cab she dipped down, seemed to be searching for the keys under the seat. Then she got it started and fishtailed in the dirt, kicking up clouds of brown dust as she peeled off. Kamau released me and I went after her.

***

I was driving the Jeep, and I was gaining on the flatbed truck that Sharia was powering. She must not have known how to drive, because she could have left me with the head start she had and with these dirt roads being as unstable as they were. She was also swerving too much, smacking the overhanging tree limbs against her windshield, trying to keep the truck steady at 60mph whereas I was doing just fine at 80mph.

The front of my Jeep had just cleared the back of her truck and we were almost side by side. I waved for her to slow down.

"Sharia, stop the truck! Talk to me!"

She hit the gas and it shot her a full car length ahead of me. I was afraid if I kept chasing her she would—

Real Bitches
Do Real Things 2

It happened just that fast. She tried to turn into a sharp curve in the road and she yanked the wheel too hard. The driver's side tires came off of the ground. I watched the whole truck turn over and go off road and down a vine-infested ravine, engine screaming as it plummeted and rolled and rolled and then slammed into a tree upside down.

"Sharia!"

I mashed on my brakes and the Jeep went skidding twenty feet—I almost went down the ravine too. I yanked up the emergency brake, hopped out and started down the ravine on foot. I was sliding on slippery rain-wet foliage. My Air Jordan sneakers weren't made for this.

"Sharia!" I yelled.

I made it to her truck and got down on my hands and knees to see inside the cab. The interior had been crushed in; the roof was smashed against the steering wheel. I looked around inside and didn't see Sharia or any sign of blood. Just shattered glass.

"Eeehh ..."

A moan, somewhere further down the hill. I got up and traveled to the sound and discovered Sharia splayed out against the base of a tree. Her head was bleeding. She was blinking at me, disoriented.

"Oohh ..." she moaned.

I pulled her arm around my neck and helped her up. "I guess it's a good thing you weren't wearing your seatbelt or you'd be dead."

Keesh

She didn't answer me. Her senses were still jumbled and she probably didn't know who I was yet. Halfway back up the ravine she started to get her footing and with her help it took less strength from me to get her back up to the road.

"Let me go!" she shouted, as she suddenly pulled away from me. She lost her balance and fell. When she tried to get back up she fell once more.

I stepped back and watched her struggle. "We're trying to help you," I said to her.

She finally got to her feet. She ran her bloody fingers through her hair as if this was really a time to look pretty.

"You're not trying to help me. You're trying to help yourself," she said to me. "I heard what yall told the governor. Yall want his cocaine plantation."

"It was never his. It's yours. It belongs to your village. We're here to liberate it."

"You're here to cash out."

"That too," I said honestly. "But I guarantee you our business will be better than his. Slavery-free. Fair profits. And there will be enough to go around. We're taking over the U.S. market."

"You're from the United States?" She asked the question like she didn't believe me.

"Yes. I'm not Spanish. Surgery just made me look this way."

Real Bitches
Do Real Things 2

She stared at me with less contempt. It was a look I'd seen before from many people I had come across. She was trying to figure out if she could use me to get ahead.

Then she said, "I'm still going back to Santa Rosa. I'm not living in a village. I'm not going back to that life."

"You don't have to. And you don't have to go back to life in Santa Rosa either. You were living it up—if you wanna call it that—in a mansion with the governor. This is the same person who put a gun to your head before he was murdered. I can only imagine the things he made you do to remain welcome in his mansion."

She looked at me fiercely. "You don't know me," she said.

"I know enough. And I see a lot in you that I saw in my last partner. She was Honduran too. You can work for me, Sharia, and see ten times as much money as the governor had. If you go back to Santa Rosa, who are you gonna cuddle with next to live the good life? Who? The mayor? A senator? Some other random man with money that'll make you do unspeakable acts just to wear a designer dress? Real bitches where I'm from make their own money, Sharia. With me and my husband, you'll be your own boss. And the United States will be your playground."

I could see in her eyes that she was weighing her options. I really wanted her to say yes. She knew the village life as well as the political life of neighboring Santa Rosa, and that could come in handy. She also had the spark of a woman-in-charge. I needed bitches like her if this pipeline was going to work for the long haul.

"You're not gonna get one kilo of that cocaine into the United States," she said.

"Why not?" I asked.

"The General won't let you."

I paused. *Was she talking about the man of folklore? The story of The General and The Queen?* Then she answered my unspoken questions.

"The governor wasn't the one who owned the plantation," she said. "He just ran it. He had a boss, and his name is General Vincente Magana. People think The General's story is myth, but he's real. I've met him. He's an active member in the *Fuerzas Militares Colombia.*"

"I thought the military wasn't involved in the drug trade down here. They have agreements with the U.S."

"That might be true. But there's corruption everywhere in Honduras. The General does whatever he wants. He pays people off. He kills people that threaten—"

A noise made us turn our heads. It was the sound of vehicles roaring close to us, but we couldn't see any cars yet because of the heavy presence of shade-bearing trees that curved with the road.

Then the first military Jeep came around the bend into sight. Then another. Then two more. Four total, all painted in army fatigue and occupied by soldiers. One of the vehicles had a World War I .50-caliber heavy machine gun mounted to it. I didn't know if we should run or not. But I knew running would get us chased and gunned down. And I never wanted to die running. My instincts told me to shoot.

I put one hand behind my back, gripping the 9mm handle sticking out of my jeans. I waited to see if they would pass us and head north to San Agustín or continue west on the route to the village.

"We need to run!" Sharia panicked. "Let's get in the Jeep and go!"

"They'll catch us," I said.

"We have to try. They're coming to the village to kill all of us!"

"How do you know?"

"The General is riding in the second car!"

One of the soldiers in the first military Jeep wore camouflage paint under his eyes. He stood up with a small black shotgun—they were closing in on us, dust billowing up as they approached—and aimed the shotgun directly at us.

"They're gonna kill us!" Sharia screamed, and she started running back down the ravine.

I watched her flee, and in that second when I turned back to the soldiers, the one with the shotgun fired at me—*I thought they had to introduce themselves first!* My left leg swept backwards unnaturally and I collapsed. My thigh was bleeding from where a buckshot got me. The pain was terrible, I clenched my teeth, and knowing I had to fight back I brought my gun around and aimed up at them. *Bang! Bang! Bang!*

I hit windshield glass and kept firing.

Bang! Bang! Bang! Bang! until my clip was empty, and then I tried to crawl back to my Jeep as they returned fire. I heard their vehicles stop. I kept crawling. Then I heard boots hit the ground, and before I knew it I was kicked and forced over on my back. My gun was snatched from me.

I stared up at a soldier with a black Ruger handgun pointed down at me. His whole face was painted in black and forest green camouflage.

Then another soldier came and stood over me too. His fatigues were decked in gold medals. He was somebody important. He wore a peak hat and had a big sweaty beard.

"My name is General Vincente Magana," he said in a heavy Spanish accent. "I will apologize for shooting you if you don't turn out to be who I'm looking for."

It's him, I thought. *This is The General!*

He turned and called for another soldier—"Laizo!" he roared—who quickly ran over with two photographs. The General took the pictures, compared them with each other, looked at me, then turned the pictures around so I could see them.

One was the picture Israel Trevino took of me in that

cabin on the hill that overlooked the plantation. Trevino must have faxed it to The General. The other picture was a mugshot of me from the Los Angeles booking where I portrayed Vida Benitez.

"Are these pictures of you?" The General asked me.

"No," I lied.

"Are my eyes playing tricks on me then?"

"No soy yo, señor," I said in Spanish. Translation: *It's not me, sir.*

He smiled, then looked at the soldier with the Ruger pointed at me. "Execute her," he commanded, then walked off.

I didn't speak as I stared up at the soldier as he jacked a round into the chamber. I had no doubt he was about to kill me.

*****

Kamau was still trying to enjoy the celebration, while at the same time thinking nonstop about his wife since the moment she took off after Sharia. He was second-guessing the drug game as a whole. With a baby on the way, life as a drug dealer would be way too dangerous. His family would be too vulnerable.

Neeta wasn't supposed to get pregnant until after they secured a pipeline. That's what they talked about and agreed on. But how could he be surprised, really? He and Neeta had sex like rabbits. He couldn't even remember what a condom felt like. They'd been so irresponsible.

And with that, he started to smile.

Sitting on a boulder a few yards away from the fire, he brought the wooden bowl of *chicha de yuca* to his lips and drank half of it.

"I'm gonna be a father," he said to himself happily, as he watched the villagers celebrate in the orange glow of the fire. "Son or daughter, I don't care. But I know Neeta's gonna want a boy."

Someone touched his bare back. He thought it was another village girl asking him to dance, until he turned and saw the old lady Antebella staring at him darkly. It startled the shit out of him.

"Destruction!" she hissed.

Kamau stood up and took a step back, dropping his bowl. "What?"

"Death!" she shrieked. Her eyes were wide open and haunting. "Death is near!"

"Old lady," Kamau began, "I don't believe in that mystical mumbo-jumbo that my wife does—"

Suddenly, the roaring of vehicles made everyone in the village stop and look. Kamau too. He saw military men in olive drab Jeeps barrel out from the forest road. One Jeep rammed into the fruit stand, crushing it, and almost hit a young woman in sandals who managed to pick up her son and get them out of the way. Another one of the Jeeps stopped in an open area of the village. This Jeep had a standard .50-caliber machine gun attached to it. The soldier behind the weapon unlatched its stabilizer, freeing it up for mobility, then gripped each handle and pointed the extended barrel down at everyone.

"Oh shit," Kamau uttered.

The soldier started firing like a mad man.

Kamau ran, everyone did. Amidst the screaming and crying—and dying—he tried to remember which shanty the assault rifles were in. He saw it, saw villagers running in and grabbing weapons and shooting back. Then there was a loud whistling and a rocket slammed into the shanty and it exploded into a big mushroom cloud of flames. A few of the villagers caught on fire.

Kamau had a 9mm in the shanty that he and Neeta had been sleeping in. He took off running for it, racing across the dirt, ducking gunfire. A village man with a wooden looped nose ring ran into him in a panic, almost knocked Kamau over. Kamau grabbed him by the shoulders.

"Did my wife come back? Have you seen her?" Kamau yelled at him.

The man's face only registered fear, and Kamau realized this was one of the villagers who didn't know English.

Bang! Bang!

Keesh

The village man's body shook twice. Then blood started to pour out of his mouth. Kamau grabbed him under the arms, trying to hold him up but there was nothing he could do. The village man was dead. Kamau let him drop to the ground, and that's when he saw the soldier directly in front of him pointing a gun at him.

Kamau raised his arms in surrender. "I'm unarmed."

Bang!

The shot knocked him off of his feet. He'd taken one to the chest, closer to his collar bone. Bleeding, he tried to stand but someone kicked him in his face. When he stopped seeing stars, he looked up into the face of one of his attackers. A military man wearing a peak hat and a thick sweaty beard put his boot on his neck.

"You must be Negro number two," the Spanish soldier said. The insignia on the lapels of his fatigues were golden and distinguishing. He was high-ranking for sure.

"I'm an American," Kamau said, breathing hard. "If you kill me, you'll have to answer to my government."

"Just as wily as the other Negro, I see. Mr. Kamau Bryant, you're a fugitive to your government. If I kill you, I get praised."

How does he know who I am? Kamau wondered.

"My name is General Vincente Magana, if you're wondering. You and your wife came into my land and murdered my people. Murdered the governor of Santa Rosa de Copán,

Real Bitches
Do Real Things 2

who was a good friend of mine. There will be no trial for you, as there was not one for your wife."

"Where's my wife?!"

"Let me show you." Vincente lifted a .357 Magnum revolver and pointed it down at Kamau's head.

"Where's my wife, muthafucka?!!"

Vincente clicked the hammer back.

"Wait!" said Laizo, who came running over.

Lowering his weapon, Vincente looked annoyed. "What is it?"

"We shouldn't kill him too. We already killed the girl."

Kamau roared and tried to get to his feet but another soldier kicked him in the face again, then put him in a headlock.

"I just received the full fax of the U.S. fugitive report," Laizo said to Vincente. "Kamau Bryant is worth a lot to us."

"Reward?"

"Yes, General."

"How much?"

"One million dollars."

Vincente wrinkled his nose, then pointed the gun back at Kamau. The soldier who had him in the headlock was trying to keep him still.

"Wait, General! He's worth more than money to us. Turning him in to the U.S. government will help

Honduras- and Colombia-United States relations. Turning him in will curry favor from the *entire world*. We need him alive."

Vincente considered it. "How bad do they want him?"

"He's number one on the America's Most Wanted list. His wife was number two. They're listed as terrorists."

"Terrorists?"

"Yes, sir. We'll be on every major news network from here to Hong Kong. The *Fuerzas Militares Colombia* will be known worldwide as heroes."

Vincente smiled, then tucked his revolver back in its holster. "Set up a press conference, Laizo. You and Fria both work together to get as many media outlets—" He cut his words off and swiftly unholstered his weapon again and pointed it across the field.

Everyone looked.

Over one hundred yards away, a surviving village boy was running to the forest in escape. The General fired once. The boy fell.

"Good shot, General," one of the soldiers said.

The General brought the muzzle to his lips and blew the smoke, cowboy style. Soldiers standing around in the huddle laughed.

"I want every media outlet known to man to be there," Vincente instructed. "I will also have to trim my beard. I must look magnificent for the people."

***

Kamau's hands were tied behind his back, as he sat in the rear of the Jeep facing the military vehicles following close behind. If he tried to roll out over the side, the trailing vehicles would either grab him and throw him back in or run over him.

On the side of the road, Kamau caught sight of the Jeep that Neeta had driven to catch Sharia. It was parked at the edge of the ravine.

"Neeta!" Kamau shouted, as he started to stand to his feet.

A soldier grabbed his legs—"Sit down, Negro!"—but Kamau stood up anyway, wobbling because they were eating up the road at least 60 mph and his hands were bound behind his back so he had no counter balance.

"Neeta!"

Just as quickly as Kamau saw the vehicle, they'd passed it and were getting further and further away. As the soldier struggled to pull him back down to a sitting position, Kamau saw a body laying beside the Jeep.

It was his wife.

"Neeta!" he screamed hysterically.

Kamau jumped out of the back of the truck and landed on his feet—for just a half of a second. He twisted his ankle and hit the dirt, smashing his forehead against the hard earth. Still, he tried to get up. But the soldiers stopped their vehicles and started piling out to grab him.

Vincente shouted, "Get him, get him! *Ándale!*"

In a team effort, the soldiers grabbed Kamau and heaved him back into the rear of the Jeep. Then they were speeding off again.

"*Loco, Negro,*" one of the soldiers laughed.

CHAPTER 18

California Hospital Medical Center
Los Angeles, California (Present Day)

Detective Figg watched the whole newscast on the Western Honduras invasion, hoping to see Kamau and Neeta's faces pop up on the screen as participants. But they never appeared. The reporters never mentioned anything about the invasion being related to cocaine—they only stated that the governor of Santa Rosa de Copán was murdered for reasons unknown; another station called the invaders "rebels"—and Figg felt silly for thinking his married suspects were there.

For all he knew, Kamau and Neeta could be hiding out in Los Angeles. Why would they try to expand their drug business when they were at the top of the FBI's list? He even heard that the CIA was involved on the case. Kamau and Neeta weren't that bold, were they?

Keesh

"I can't wait till I catch you guys," Figg said to himself, still standing in the center of the waiting room staring at the television. "There's still a lot of questions I need answered."

He turned and started back down the hall to Hershey's room. The nurse should have been done by now, and Detective Figg had a few more questions for the Crenshaw Mafia leader.

When he walked back in the room, Hershey Moore was sitting up in the bed putting on a Crenshaw Cougars high school sweater.

"Going somewhere?" Figg asked him.

"No, sir. Just getting cold."

Figg thought that Hershey should have been handcuffed. But legally it wasn't possible. Hershey's health was in danger, and certain physical safeguards had been put in place in 1996 by the HIPAA act that prevented him from being restrained.

Figg sat down. "Do you think Neeta still has the same looks? With all the speculation surrounding her and plastic surgery, do you think she went and changed her appearance again?"

"I don't think so. She knows if she keeps fucking around in those operating rooms she'll start looking like a warthog."

"Have you ever spoken to her about her surgeries?"

"No."

"Never?"

"I might've made a joke in passing, saying she's doing too much. That's about it. Most people change aliases—she changed faces. I didn't think she should be messing around with those doctors. I miss her natural beauty. But I guess it worked in her favor. She fooled yall into thinking she was Vida."

Figg still felt embarrassed by that. He had Neeta in his palms, and he unknowingly let that cunning bitch walk free.

"But I did talk to Murk one time about Neeta getting surgery," Hershey added.

"What did he say?"

"We were high, high as fuck, so I don't know if he was kidding or not. But for Neeta's 16th birthday he said he was getting her a Mercedes-Benz, and also an extra special breast enhancement."

"What was so extra special about it?"

"He said he was gonna have the doctors install Kevlar into her chest. Bulletproof breasts. I laughed my ass off."

Figg's cellphone rang. He fished it out of the inside pocket of his suit jacket, saw Stephen Beck on the ID and answered it.

"Hello?"

"I need you down in Honduras now!" the chief of police hollered.

Keesh

"Okay, what for?" Figg asked in a hopeful voice, as he stood up and walked away from Hershey.

"Our suspect Kamau Bryant has been apprehended by the *Fuerzas Militares Colombia*. There's some general named Vincente Magana claiming to have captured him single-handedly. Right now they're holding a press conference and haven't released any pictures of Mr. Bryant. But we still believe it's legit."

Figg went into the bathroom and locked himself inside. "What about Neeta Bryant?"

"They haven't said anything about her. But fuck her! I want Kamau Bryant!"

"Plane tickets?"

"Already handled. Check your email. You'll be accompanying the U.S. Marshalls down to Western Honduras to pick him up. I need you at LAX now!"

"Yes, sir. Thank you, sir."

Figg hung up, yanked the bathroom door open and stepped out, stuffing his cellphone back in his inside pocket—when he suddenly stopped.

Hershey was gone.

"Sonofabitch ..."

He ran over to the side of the bed and cursed again. His tape recorder was gone too.

"Fuck! Fuck! Fuck!"

Real Bitches Do Real Things 2

The window was open. It led onto the hospital roof. Figg crawled out onto it, then pulled out his police-issued Glock .40 as he raced across the white-capped roof in the cold. He ran to the edge of the roof and looked down.

It was a two-story drop, but low enough for a man to survive it. Hershey must have jumped. And somebody must have been waiting for him below.

"And you took my fucking tape recorder with you, you bastard."

Disappointed in himself, Figg holstered his gun and put his hands on his hips as he stared across the hospital's south parking lot.

"I can't believe I got outsmarted again," he mumbled. "Sonofafuckingbitch ..."

CHAPTER 19

Western Honduras

7 miles outside The Village (Present Day)

Sharia had been hiding in the woods for hours. She didn't start making her way back to the road until it got dark and it started to rain.

The hill was extra slick now, and at times Sharia found herself crawling up it.

"*Oh, la mierda,*" she gasped when she saw Neeta laying on the side of the road. Neeta's leg had been shot, and she'd also taken a bullet to the chest.

In the pouring rain, Sharia knelt down beside Neeta's body and checked her neck for a pulse. She thought she felt one, but couldn't be sure because her fingers were wet and cold.

Then Sharia did something she hadn't done in forever—she decided to help somebody. She pulled Neeta by one arm, dragging her across the soggy ground to the Jeep.

Sharia had seen plenty men and women in the same state as Neeta and didn't help a single one. The governor ordered numerous executions in his mansion and Sharia had witnessed half of them because she was one of the governor's main concubines. She could have helped several escape, or assist them in stopping their bleeding but she hadn't. She didn't care.

But for some reason she cared about Neeta. Maybe because Neeta offered to help her, give a bitch a job. No strings attached.

"If you're alive, the village doctor will help you," Sharia said to Neeta's unmoving body that lay across the back seat. "He's the best in the country."

Sharia drove back to the village, and she wasn't surprised to see numerous dead bodies laying all over the grass, spread out in the dirt, women who had lived through the massacre crying next to the deceased, a young boy slumped against a stone wall who looked to be sleeping but the grisly streaks of blood painted all over his skin said otherwise.

The General was a merciless man. It was no secret. The world had heard his story.

Sharia parked the Jeep and asked two men to help her get Neeta out of the back and into the village doctor's shanty. One of the men looked like he'd been shot himself but he still grabbed Neeta under the arms and the other grabbed her legs. Sharia held the shanty door open and the men laid Neeta on a wood operating table.

The doctor, who wore an unbuttoned shirt that exposed his bony chest, touched the chain around Neeta's neck. He lifted it, examining the image of the seventh-century queen Lady K'abel. "How long has she been in this state, Sharia?"

"Over five hours."

"Then I must work fast."

The doctor took his shirt off, climbed on top of Neeta's body and stuck his knife inside her chest, fishing around for the bullet with the tip of his blade. He found the bullet, removed it, then asked Sharia in Spanish to hand him a smaller knife, which he used to make a U-shaped incision on her breast. He folded the flap of skin down and stuck both of his bloody hands into her body and removed some kind of large, soft material. Sharia was puzzled by it; it looked man-made. The doctor looked confused by it too.

"What is it?" Sharia asked him.

"I don't know," he replied. "But it stopped the bullet from hitting her vitals."

"Is she going to live?"

"I believe so, Sharia. Lady K'abel has come back to us ..."

The following is an excerpt from:

Real Bitches Do Real Things 3

1

Western Honduras
Santa Rosa de Copán

Detective Figg extended his hand to The General. "My name is Detective Matt Figg. Nice to make your acquaintance, sir."

The General shook his hand firmly. "General Vincente Magana. Are you ready to see your fugitive?"

"Certainly."

They were at the police station in Santa Rosa de Copán, heading downstairs where the holding cells were located. Two U.S. Marshals accompanied Figg, and one soldier walked ahead with The General. This headquarters had no air conditioning at all, as far as Figg could tell. He was very tempted to take off his blazer and sling it over his shoulder, but that would have been unprofessional. So he beared it, wiping his forehead sweat on a handkerchief, as they descended further into the basement. It was dark, just a few light bulbs overhead, and it seemed to get darker the further down they went. These conditions for prisoners wouldn't fly in the United States. Human rights advocates would have had a field day. But here in Honduras it seemed rights were ostensibly ignored.

Keesh

At ground level, they started across a long hall lit with more weak light bulbs. They passed a few empty cells.

To get his mind off of the heat, Figg tried to start conversation. "Excuse me, General. How long have you been in the military?"

The General kept leading the way. "Too long, Detective. Way too long."

"Got kids?"

"A daughter. Why?"

"Just asking. I heard a lot of stories about a Honduran General who had a daughter named The Queen. They took over a cocaine plantation together and started trafficking drugs to the U.S. I was wondering if you were that general, because I think my fugitive came down here chasing that story."

The General gave off a grunt, and Figg took that as a laugh. "No, I'm afraid I'm not that general. But you're not the first to ask me that. Mostly kids do. There are no cocaine plantations in Honduras. My military cleared them all out. If your fugitive was looking for cocaine, he should have gone to Bolivia."

"There was actually another fugitive that was reportedly in this area as well. Her name is Neeta Bryant. She's Kamau Bryant's wife."

"Haven't seen her, Detective. But if she's in my country, she will be found."

"She might be harder to find than Kamau. His wife doesn't look African-American. She looks more Latin than anything, and she's also a good liar."

The General stopped and shined his flashlight into a dark cell. He said, "Here's the only fugitive I have."

Figg stepped forward and looked inside the cell. The prisoner was squinting from the bright light shining in his face but Figg recognized him. This was Kamau Bryant. His dreads were a lot longer than what the pictures in the LAPD's non-public database showed, but that was to be expected. What Figg _didn't_ expect was for Kamau to be so bloody. He had a fat lip and a puffy eye. But Figg wasn't about to question General Vincente Magana's methods in apprehending and detaining criminals. The good thing was Kamau was still alive and able to stand trial.

Chief of Police Stephen Beck was going to be a happy camper.

***

Kamau's hands were cuffed in the front with Detective Figg's handcuffs. Figg was holding onto his arm, standing behind him but still guiding him toward their assigned plane seats.

"Window view or aisle?" Figg asked his detainee.

Keesh

Kamau didn't respond. He just stood there in the aisle staring down at his new orange jumpsuit, completely lost in thought. His long dreads were hanging and nearly covering his whole face. He hadn't said a word since Figg pulled him out of that vile cell in Santa Rosa.

"You get window then."

They sat, and across the aisle the U.S. marshals sat. Figg pulled out his smartphone and sent a text to Stephen Beck to let him know they made it on the commercial airline safely. Figg didn't touch any other device until the plane was in the air.

He pulled out a new tape recorder and set it on his left thigh.

"Can you answer a couple questions for me, Mr. Bryant?" Figg asked.

Kamau was staring out of the window at the clouds. Again, he didn't say a thing.

"Whatever you say to me will be taken into consideration," Figg said. "You're looking at the death penalty. Hershey already told me everything. This is your only chance to save yourself."

Figg was still staring at the back of Kamau's head. The fugitive wouldn't turn away from the tiny window.

"I guess this means you're content with the death penalty," Figg said.

No response.

"Did you find the cocaine plantation you were looking for?"

Nothing. No movement whatsoever.

"Where's your wife, Kamau? Huh? Where's Neeta?"

Kamau turned and looked Figg dead in the eyes with a meanness that could kill. Then he turned back to the window.

Figg didn't know what that look was for, but he knew he hit a sweet spot. He was going to get Kamau Bryant to talk, one way or another. He had time. They had a long plane ride ahead of them.

Text **JORDAN** to **77948**

And stay updated on all of Jordan Belcher Presents' *newest releases, free giveaways,* and *special promotions!*

ON SALE NOW!

www.felonybooks.com

CPSIA information can be obtained
at www.ICGtesting.com
Printed in the USA
LVOW10s1601160217
524502LV00001B/180/P